RANGER

K.M. NEUHOLD
NORA PHOENIX

Ranger by K.M. Neuhold and Nora Phoenix

Copyright ©2020 K.M. Neuhold and Nora Phoenix

Cover design: Quinn Ward

Editing: Tanja Ongkiehong

All rights reserved. No part of this story may be used, reproduced, or transmitted in any form by any means without the written permission of the copyright holder, except in case of brief quotations and embodied within critical reviews and articles.

This is a work of fiction. Names, characters, places, and incidents either are the products of the author's imagination or are used fictitiously. Any resemblance to actual persons, living or dead, businesses, companies, events, or locales is entirely coincidental. The use of any real company and/or product names is for literary effect only. All other trademarks and copyrights are the property of their respective owners.

This book contains sexually explicit material which is suitable only for mature readers.

1
RANGER

I'm fucked.

It's the only conclusion I can reach as I sit on my porch, the sweat on my body slowly evaporating, as I empty my bottle of Heineken. Butterflies are dancing over the yellow primroses and red poppies in my wild garden, and the first crickets are singing their mating song in the quiet of my little piece of what was supposed to be heaven. The air is still warm, but the breeze brushes my skin, promising a night that's at least a little cooler in the last days of spring. Lord knows we won't get any relief during the summer.

I inhale deeply, but even the comforting smell of lavender from the countless big pots on my porch can't soothe me. Nothing can.

I'm fucked big-time.

It's been a year since I was honorably discharged, and all the yoga and meditation in the world haven't made a lick of difference. I still can't sleep, still have trouble eating. And the nightmares are still there, even when I don't sleep. All I have to do is close my eyes, and I see it again. See him again.

It has got to stop. I've had enough of this. I refuse to be this moping, sad guy who served his country well once upon a time but then descended into a pit of despair and never managed to climb out of it again. I *can't* be that person.

I thought that the discharge would help, that being here on my peaceful little ranch would magically fix me. It didn't. And neither did anything else I tried.

The yoga certainly helps me keep flexible, but it didn't bring the peace of mind I had hoped for. Neither did meditating. Or herbal tea. Essential oils. Eating goddamn kale. Name any new age method spouted by gurus, and I've tried it. I even went so far as to try sunning my asshole... Yeah, not doing that one again.

It. Doesn't. Work.

I have little bursts where I'll feel better, and I'll tackle the garden or vacuum the house, and it'll look nice for a week or so. But inevitably, that boost disappears just as fast as it popped up, and I'll be fighting with myself to find the energy to put a pizza in the oven. My body, once a strong, efficient soldier, is now nothing but tired muscles and weak bones, held together by a frame that's at least twenty pounds too thin.

So I've finally decided to stop trying all the vague methods and go for a proven one. I call my brother Lucky. I hate this, hate that as his older brother, I'm the weaker one, but I've reached a point where I have no other choice. And the one thing I'm certain of is that he would never turn me away...and that he'd never judge me.

He answers on the third ring.

"Hey, bro," he says, his voice steady as a rock. Lucky is like that. Unflappable. Strong. Someone I can lean on, even though he's two years younger than me. He's always had my back, and I know he's been worried about me.

"I need help," I say, forgoing all small talk.

His two men are talking in the background—and yes, my brother has two partners. Lucky bastard. They're both amazing too. Mason is super sweet and dorky, and Heart is the sexiest guy I've ever seen. Both love Lucky with all they have...and that's mutual. Somehow, they're making their threesome work.

But if I ask how Mason and Heart are doing, I'll lose the courage to pour my heart out. Besides, Lucky and I talked a week or two ago, and I doubt anything happened between then and now. Otherwise, he'd have called me.

"I'm here. What do you need?"

"How do I fix this? How do I fix me?"

The voices in the background grow dimmer. Lucky must've walked away from them. "Am I interrupting?" I'm not even sure if I hope he'll say yes so I can hang up and forget about the whole thing.

"You know you're not. I could be in the middle of a blow job or balls deep in one of my men, and I'd still take your call."

My mouth pulls up at the corners at that blunt visual. "Thanks for putting that image in my head."

"You're welcome. Now, back to you. You gotta tell me what needs to be fixed—and note my strong objection to that term."

"Noted. I don't know how else to put it."

"Talk to me, Mack," Lucky says, his voice soft. Gone is the teasing man, and in its place is the worried brother. He even uses my real name. He knows I'm in serious shit.

How I want to tell him everything, but even the thought of the man I lost, the mere mention of his name, sends my heart into a wild frenzy, and at the edges of my vision, the darkness is creeping in. I summon up all my training not to break down in front of my brother. I have enough pride left for that.

"I can't talk," I say between clenched teeth. "Not about what happened. But I need help. I've been diagnosed with…"

Dammit, why can't I even say those stupid four letters? Why is it so hard for me to admit this? It's not my fault, I'm far from the only one, and it doesn't say anything about me not being strong enough or some macho bullshit. I *know* all that, and still, it's so goddamn hard. I punch my right thigh, my leg bouncing like a rocking horse.

"…with PTSD," Lucky finishes for me.

Of course he knew already. He's not stupid, and besides, he's a former Marine. Pretty sure my parents have recognized the symptoms as well. My dad was a Marine too, so he must've seen this before from his former team members.

I take a deep breath in through my nose, then exhale slowly through my mouth. "Yes."

"I'm sorry…" Lucky's voice, full of concern and love, penetrates the dark fog in my head, and some of the tension in my shoulders eases. I uncurl my fist and let it rest on my now still leg. I have the best brother in the world; I really do, and the fact that I recognize that even in the darkness I'm in speaks volumes about how true that statement is.

"I know."

"What can I do?"

"I've tried everything. I need something to help me get through the days, to help me sleep, to keep the darkness at bay… Fuck, I even tried group therapy, but you know I'm not a talker. Besides, being around other people is…not good right now."

"I have a suggestion."

I narrow my eyes and swat at a persistent fly buzzing around my head. "Already?"

"I've been waiting for you to call me for a year."

"Yeah, I know. I'm sorry. I..." I pinch between my eyebrows. "What's your idea?"

"There's an organization called Pups for Patriots, and they provide therapy dogs to vets. These dogs are specifically trained to help vets, for example, with PTSD. They sense your stress or when you're in distress, and they can help calm you down."

A dog. Oh god, yes. The idea of having to talk to people is enough to make me break out in a sweat, but a dog is a different story. I love dogs; I always have. I could never have one myself, what with me being in the Army and all, but my parents have always had dogs—German shepherds, a husky, some mixed labs.

"How do I know if I qualify for one?"

"You do."

"How can you be so sure?" As soon as I've asked the question, I know the answer. "You already contacted them."

"I have connections. You know Cameron, former Ballsy Boy Campy, who Heart worked with? His boyfriend is Jackson Criswell, the TV star. I met him at a Ballsy Boys get-together, and we got to chat. He works with this animal trainer for the show he's shooting, and that guy is the volunteer trainer for Pups for Patriots in your area. I already called him, and he's ready to talk to you. His name is Julian Barnes. I'll text you his contact info."

My tired brain needs a few seconds to figure out the connections. Heart, one of my brother's boyfriends, used to work for the Ballsy Boys studio as a porn star, so that's how he knows Campy. Of course I know Campy as well, albeit only from his videos. He's retired now, as is Heart—though

I've never watched his videos again after learning my brother had a thing for him, a thing that has developed into a beautiful relationship. But that's how my down-to-earth brother got to hang out with one of Hollywood's hottest new TV stars.

I chuckle. "Damn, look at you being all connected. And wow, you really did come prepared."

"I've been sitting on this, waiting for you to be ready. And that's not an accusation or a complaint, you know that. This is your journey, and you'll walk it at your pace, but I wanted to be there when you asked for help."

My throat closes up unexpectedly, and I swallow. "Thank you. I—"

"Don't. I love you. I'm here."

That simple statement perfectly sums up our relationship. When we were both serving, he in the Marines and I with the Army Rangers, staying in touch was a challenge at times. We've had months when we couldn't talk to each other. But one thing had always been a constant: he was there if I needed him and vice versa.

"I'll call him and see what he can do for me."

"Good. I'll call you tomorrow evening to hear what he said."

A laugh bubbles up. "You're still as bossy as ever. I don't know how your men put up with you."

"I give really good head."

I'm still grinning when I end the call.

A dog. I feel lighter, as if a tiny ray of sunshine has chased away the deepest darkness inside me. I'll call this Julian guy tomorrow.

2

JULIAN

My entire adolescence, I only wanted one thing —a dog. I checked out every breed-specific book and training guide in our extensive library, and I would just about cut a bitch if my family tried to change the channel off Animal Planet while *K-9 to Five* was on. I was not messing around. The only problem was, my mom seemed to think we were, and I quote, "not dog people."

As I step out of my bedroom to my pack of exceptionally well-trained, soon-to-be-placed-in-new-homes service dogs, all I can think is how very much my mom didn't get me. The dog thing is just the start, but I digress...

Princess Pinecone, my very sweet, ancient husky, who had the misfortune of being named by my niece, who was five at the time, harrumphs as she ambles out of the bedroom, hot on my heels. Most mornings, she's not impressed with the rest of the dogs who greet us on the other side of the bedroom door. Which is very unfair of her. After all, they don't jump or bark; they don't chew things or mess in the house. They *do* shed quite a bit, but considering the tufts of hair PP leaves around, I don't think she has any room to judge anyone else.

I yawn, patting each of the dogs on the head and greeting them by name so none of them feel jealous or neglected. Calzone, Benny, Rita, Lila, and Theodore came to me for training just over a year ago, all from the same litter of golden retrievers.

"Time for breakfast, my dudes," I announce, and they all politely wag their tails and beeline for the kitchen. Well, all except for PP, who bulldozes through the rest of the gang to get to the front of the line. What's that saying about your own kids always behaving the worst? I may have the skills to train horses to star in film and TV and dogs to service disabled vets, but no one, and I mean *no one,* can tell a thirteen-year-old husky what to do.

I shuffle after them and hit the button on the coffee maker, then go through my routine of filling six bowls and setting each down in front of the dogs, sitting still until they're released to eat. Even PP obeys this rule because she knows the food comes right after.

Once the dogs are all chowing down, I grab my phone from the counter, where I accidentally left it last night, and open my calendar app to check my schedule for the day while I wait for my coffee to finish brewing.

Today won't be too busy. A call in the afternoon with a producer who needs a horse for some TV drama series. And this morning, I have an appointment with a veteran who's interested in learning about getting a service dog.

"One of you kiddos might be getting booted out of here to a new home soon," I inform the dogs, who all look at me but don't seem too concerned with the information. They may not mind, but a pang hits me in the center of my chest. Training service dogs is infinitely rewarding and extremely fulfilling, but sending them off to a new home when the time comes never gets any easier. If everything goes according to plan, they all will be placed within the next month or so, and I'll start all over with a new batch. The new puppy stage is fun but *much* louder and messier than when they're fully trained. PP hates it.

Once I'm fully caffeinated, I head outside to get a start on feeding the horses. I barely have the front door open when a loud bray pierces my eardrums.

"For the love of all that's holy, Doc, your breakfast is coming," I shout back, even though it's useless. Doc is as deaf as a doorknob. PP immediately trots off, but the other five dogs wait for my release signal, then go about their business and stretch their legs.

As I step into the barn, the familiar, comforting smell of hay and horse hits me. Some may call the scent an acquired taste, but I just call it home. The horses rattle their stall doors, and Doc brays loudly again. I feed him first. He's been known to finagle his stall open if I make him wait too long. How he does it is a mystery. I'm half convinced he's not a donkey at all but an interdimensional sorcerer. Or just really smart. Whichever.

I whistle as I go about my morning chores of feeding all my furry kiddos. Then I turn them loose so I can clean the barn. After the horses, I tend to the chickens and finally, my one lone goat, which I was supposed to train for a movie, but goats make huskies look like honor students by comparison. Butler is my nemesis, and he knows it.

I dodge his horns as I fill his trough with alfalfa hay and then open the door that leads out to the horse pasture. He likes to hang out with the horses; he just doesn't like me. I'm not sure why. I'm a rather friendly guy if he'd give me half a chance.

With all that done, I have just enough time to grab a shower before hopping into my truck.

Half an hour later, I pull slowly into the long driveway leading up to the house, gravel crunching under my tires. I park and double-check the notes I made after the phone call last night.

When I first answered the phone, silence greeted me on the other end of the line, and I'd figured whoever was calling had gotten a wrong number and hung up. But right when I was about to end the call, a thready, quiet voice had come through the phone.

He told me his name was Ranger and that I'd spoken to his brother Lucky. Things clicked into place from there. Lucky had called me months ago, asking a lot of pointed questions about how my dogs could help veterans suffering from PTSD. We'd had a good chat about things, and he'd said he'd pass the information along. When I didn't hear anything, I figured the brother simply wasn't interested. Now I'm thinking it might've been a little more serious than that.

I hop out of my truck, glancing around at the unkempt property. The grass is long, and the roof looks like it might be one bad storm away from caving in. But it also seems the front door has a fresh cover of paint, so maybe he's working on it? I give him the benefit of the doubt. I stride up to the door, bracing myself for whatever might be waiting on the other side. Over the years, I've seen it all from vets who were mostly getting by but needed a little extra emotional support to those who looked like they might fall apart at any second, and everything in between.

I rap at the door. Within seconds, footsteps thump on the other side. I step back from the door and keep my hands out of my pockets, plastering on a big smile so I look as nonthreatening as possible; all things I've discovered over the years of working with vets dealing with extreme cases of PTSD.

The door swings open. Fiddlesticks, he's *hot*. He's pale and a bit skinny and looks like he hasn't showered in a few days, but still, I wouldn't kick him out of bed.

Sadly, this isn't Grindr, and I'm not here to drool over the dark-eyed man with the strong jaw and surprisingly long eyelashes.

"Hi, I'm Julian with Pups for Patriots," I introduce myself, slowly extending my hand. I learned my lesson the first time I came on way too strong, thrusting my hand out with all the enthusiasm god gave me and nearly triggered the poor woman into an attack. Since then, I'm always careful to keep a tight lid on my eagerness, especially during the initial meeting.

"Ranger," he answers, his voice clipped but not unfriendly. Guarded, that's what it is.

He leads me into the living room, and luckily for everyone involved, the inside looks somewhat better kept than the outside would suggest. Not great, mind you, but not unlivable either. I take a seat on the couch he shows me to and pull my clipboard with the questionnaire out of my messenger bag.

"Like I explained on the phone last night, I'm going to start by asking some questions if that's okay?" Ranger grunts and nods. "Do you have any physical injuries or disabilities? An amputation or a head injury that could result in seizures, anything of that nature?"

"No." Ranger shakes his head. "Do I not qualify without a physical injury?"

"Oh no, no, that's not it at all," I assure him. "Part of what

I'm trying to do today is to assess your specific needs so I can pair you with the right dog."

"The right dog?" he repeats, sounding skeptical.

"Yes. While any dog can be a great companion, some of them specialize in alerting for a seizure or reacting appropriately when one happens. Others are best for aiding with stability as needed if you have a prosthetic, and so on. I've trained five dogs personally for different demands of care and support and have access to more through the organization if needed," I explain.

"I can see how a dog would help with those things." He cards his hands through his messy hair. "But I don't get how it's going to help with the fucked-up shit going on inside my head."

"I'm glad you asked. First, it's psychologically proven that having a nonjudgmental companion like a dog can be extremely comforting. Their presence even causes endorphins to release in our brains when they're near. But more than that, the dogs I train can detect the initial signs of a PTSD attack. The increased heart rate and breathing, sudden tension, even a spike in blood pressure are all detectable to them.

"When your dog notices you're about to have an episode, they'll start by leaning into you, then lick your hand. For many people, the weight of a dog's body is a great grounding technique. You can run your fingers through their fur and talk to them. All these things can pull you out of it. If this isn't enough, they can take the next step, getting between you and any other people in the room to keep both you and others safe. They can go as far as herding you away from a situation or environment. During the night, they're also vigilant, able to wake you safely from a nightmare and then use these same comforting techniques I just described."

I've made this pitch to potential recipients a hundred times, but it never stops being powerful to me when their expression morphs from skeptical to hopeful in just a few sentences.

"They can do all that?" he asks quietly as if he's afraid to hope *too* much.

"And more."

3

RANGER

I stare at Julian for way longer than can be considered polite, but I'm speechless. When Lucky told me about this Pups for Patriots program, I thought I'd be getting a well-behaved dog who would keep me company. A buddy, someone to force me to keep going because he'd be dependent on me. But that would be it. A dog. But what Julian describes takes it to a whole new level. It's hard for me to believe it could be true, but if it is...

I clear my throat. "And vets are saying this helps them?"

Julian nods enthusiastically. When he smiles, his whole face lights up as if the sun comes through. "I'm happy to provide you with a contact number from a veteran who has benefitted from our program. We've helped hundreds of veterans find their perfect dog, and all their lives have been better for it."

"How do you decide which dog would work for someone?"

"That's what this intake interview is for. My goal is to get to know you a little and learn about your day-to-day life so I can assess which dog would be the best fit for you. Like I said, I've trained five dogs, so those would have first dibs on you, but if I feel none of them match, I have more options from other trainers."

First dibs on me? As if the dog chooses me instead of the other way around. It's a strange thought that's scary and comforting at the same time.

"Can you tell me what a typical day looks like for you?" Julian asks.

I sigh. "I get up at oh-six-hundred. Years of being in the Army have programmed my body for that."

"What did you do in the Army?"

"I'm an Army Ranger. I *was* an Army Ranger," I correct myself. It stings to speak of my life's passion in the past tense, but I've accepted that that part of my life is over.

"Okay. And what do you do during the day? Do you have a job outside of the home?"

I shake my head. "No. I start with yoga... It supposedly helps. Then breakfast and then I work on whatever I can muster the energy for. The garden, renovating the house, endless rounds of bureaucracy and paperwork with the VA. Sometimes, I take a nap in the afternoon."

Lately, it's been my routine most days because for some reason, my nightmares aren't as bad during the day as they are at night. I rarely sleep more than two, three hours, so by the time lunch rolls around, I'm exhausted, and after eating something, I fall asleep on the couch.

"I try to do more." Can I sound any more like a total bum who idles the day away? Not that I should care what Julian thinks of me, but he seems so put together and professional, and I'm two steps away from being the epitome of a sad fuck. God knows I already look the part. "But my energy has been...unreliable."

He holds up a hand. "Please don't feel like you have to

defend yourself. There's no judgment from me. But knowing where your energy level is at helps me choose the best dog for you. For example, Calzone, one of the dogs available, is a high-energy dog who loves to play and go for walks. He wouldn't be a good fit for you, whereas I've got some more mellow pups that would suit you much better."

"What you're looking for is a retired Greyhound dog. One of those dogs that wants to do nothing but sleep on the couch all day. That's about my energy level," I say dryly.

Julian smiles, and I look away. He's cute, and it makes me painfully aware that I'm the mayor of Loserville. Pathetic doesn't even cut it, and yet as fast as that thought pops up, I realize just as quickly that as much as I regret it, I lack the capability to do something about it. Not that I'm interested in being attractive or anything like that. I had my chance at love, and I fucking ruined it.

"From what you tell me, it does sound like you can keep a daily schedule of some kind. That's important because your dog will depend on you to feed and walk him...or let him outside. Which reminds me. Your garden isn't fenced in. Would you be willing to put a fence up so he or she would be able to play outside? And I mean a real fence, not an electric one. They're not suitable for—"

"Absolutely not." Julian stares at me, eyes wide, mouth agape. "An electric fence, I mean. I know some people swear by them, but I hate the idea. I can put up a fence...if you give me some time."

Julian flashes me one of his happy smiles. "Of course. And do you have any experience with dogs or other pets?"

"We always had dogs growing up, so yes."

"What kinds of dogs?"

"All kinds. Some mixed labs, a husky—"

"I've got a husky. PP is the most stubborn, opinionated dog you'll ever meet, but she's amazing."

The way he talks about her is sweet, his face radiating his affection for her. A tiny flicker of hope sparks inside me. Maybe, just maybe, I can bond with a dog like that and find comfort in having a companion. But what if none of the dogs like me? What if they sense the darkness in me and are repelled by that? My flash of joy and happiness is doused just as fast.

"Does it ever happen that it doesn't work out? That a dog doesn't like the vet?"

Julian cocks his head as he studies me, his eyes kind but serious. "Rarely, but if it does, we try again with a different dog. And in some cases, we opt for a slower process where the vet and the dog hang out a few times before he or she takes the dog in permanently. Are you worried about that?"

God, how do I answer that? I hate lying on principle, but I have no intention of sharing my darkest, deepest thoughts with him. He'd bolt out the door faster than the aforementioned Greyhound, and fuck knows they can *run*.

I clear my throat. "Just wondering if dogs can get affected by someone's moods. I'd hate to make a dog depressed."

Julian sends me an encouraging smile. "I honestly don't think that's even possible. Most dogs are pure rays of sunshine that will love you no matter what, and I know for a fact that's true for the five I have right now."

A little more reassured, I answer the rest of his questions, and he's got quite a few of them. When we're done, he asks for a tour through the house.

I hesitate. "I wasn't counting on that."

Yes, that's politely worded code for "It's a godawful mess,

and I'd be embarrassed to show my mother this, let alone a complete stranger."

"There's no need to be uncomfortable. I just want to check if your house needs any adjustments to make it dog-proof."

I didn't think it was still possible to blush at the ripe age of thirty-six, but my cheeks heat up as I get up and lead him through my house. How fucking embarrassing to have someone else see the sad state of my house. When I bought it, I was so proud, so determined to fix it up and make it shine. One day, maybe, but definitely not yet.

It's reasonably clean, since I had an energy boost ten or so days ago and attacked half the house with Mr. Clean lemon spray. I haven't done jack shit since, but at least dust and grime don't cover every surface, so there's that.

Julian doesn't say anything as I show him my bedroom, where piles of clean clothes are on the floor everywhere, the bathroom, with heaps of dirty clothes, and two guest rooms, with a mountain of unopened boxes. Some of them have been packed up since I enlisted, and I don't even know what's in there.

"Do you do this full time?" I ask, desperate to distract him. Lucky told me something about Julian working with animals in another capacity, but I can't quite remember. One of the side effects of my PTSD is that my short-term memory sucks.

"Training dogs for Pups for Patriots? No. I am a full-time animal trainer, though."

I frown. "Animal trainer? What does that mean?"

"I train animals for movies or TV. Mostly dogs and horses, but I've worked with some other animals as well, including a goat."

"A goat? Can you even train those?"

Julian laughs, a full-out laugh that fills the room. "I'd have to say no wholeheartedly, but god knows I tried. Butler is the bane of my existence, but I've always loved a challenge."

"How many animals do you have?"

"I have my own husky, Princess Pinecone, or PP for short, and then five dogs, plus Butler the goat, a donkey, five horses, and a bunch of chickens."

"Wow. That's a lot."

He shrugs. "I love working with animals."

Yeah, that much is clear from the passionate way he talks about his menagerie.

"You have two outlets in the bedroom that aren't properly covered, so make sure to fix those," Julian says, and that's the only critical remark he makes. Props to his poker face, which never showed a trace of disgust or shock when we walked through the house. I appreciate that more than I can express.

"Does that mean I passed the test?"

I really hope that didn't come out as fucking pathetic as it sounded to my own ears, but Julian flashes me another one of his happy smiles. He said his dogs are rays of sunshine, but he's damn bright and shiny himself. "Absolutely. I'll contact you in a day or two with a proposal for a dog, and we can set up a first meet and see if you fit. How does that sound?"

I nod, unable to speak. I'm scared to even hope, but somewhere deep inside me, a tiny seed has grown roots that perhaps a dog could make a difference. They don't call them man's best friends for nothing.

4

JULIAN

I feel a little bit like a parent driving their kid to preschool for the first time as I near Ranger's house for a second time, except parents know they're getting to bring their kid back home at the end of the day. Benny is buckled into the passenger seat of my truck, wagging his tail, his tongue lolling out as he watches the scenery fly by outside the window.

"Now, don't be nervous," I advise. "No pressure to click with him or anything. Just go with your gut."

He huffs in what I assume is agreement. He's a dog; he doesn't have to be told twice about trusting his instincts.

"He's pretty cute." I grin just a little at the memory of Ranger's cautiously hopeful, not-quite smile I finally earned by the end of our meeting yesterday. "Not that you care." Of course he doesn't care. That's why dogs are so great. "Obviously, I'm not *interested* in him. I'm just making conversation. He's probably not gay anyway." Another fantastic thing about dogs: they never complain when you ramble.

His driveway comes into view, and I slow to pull in.

Benny whines softly, on full alert now that he realizes we're not just out for a drive but actually going somewhere new.

"Just be yourself, and I'm sure he'll love you." I put the truck in Park and pat Benny's silky head. Last night, I gave him a nice bubble bath and spritzed him with doggy cologne so he'd be presentable for today.

I start to climb out of the truck and spot Ranger a few yards away, shirtless in the bright midmorning sun, his thin body glistening with sweat, hefting a large post upright. It takes me a few seconds to realize what he's doing. Figgy pudding, is he building the fence by hand?

I rush around to Benny's side of the truck, open the door, unbuckle his harness from the seat belt, and step back so he can jump out. Then I jog toward Ranger, high-stepping through the tall grass, with the dog right on my heels.

"Ranger," I say his name carefully as we approach. He looks over his shoulder, wiping his arm across his forehead and glancing from me to Benny, a partial smile tilting the corner of his mouth. "I'm sorry. I hope you didn't think I meant that you should build a fence yourself." I gesture to the half-erected fence. I didn't notice it. I was so focused on getting over to him, but there are several other perimeter posts already in place. Has he been working on this all morning?

He shrugs, removing his work gloves and tucking them into the back pocket of his worn, dirty jeans. He might be skinny, but he has a damn nice ass. Not that I'm looking. That would be inappropriate and unprofessional. But if I *were* looking, I'd note how taut those glorious glutes seem to be in the old pair of jeans clinging to him for dear life.

"Is this my dog?" he asks, looking curiously at Benny again, who has inched closer to him in the most polite canine way imaginable. His nose twitches, but he's not overly obvious about getting Ranger's scent as he sidles up next to him. That he went to Ranger instead of staying by my side is a good sign. It means he's picking up on the important things he should recognize to form a strong bond between them, namely that this is a human deeply in need of his doggy expertise.

"If the two of you click, he can be." I smile when he offers his hand for Benny to get a proper sniff. "I'd love to give the two of you a chance to get to know each other a little, and if things feel right, I'll show you the commands he knows and go over his care instructions."

He shifts, the smallest amount of tension filling him, but Benny notices it too and reacts by licking Ranger's fingers and wagging his tail. Ranger's mouth twitches again in that almost smile, and I do an internal happy dance. They're bonding!

It doesn't always happen this quickly, but it's beautiful when it does. He strokes his fingers through the dog's fur, his shoulders relaxing little by little.

"So...you'd leave him here today? And then I'd be responsible for him from here on out?"

"If you don't think you're ready for that, we can work on a more gradual schedule. But I find that the strongest bonds occur when the dog understands as quickly as possible that *you* are his human. He has a pack bond with me and the other dogs, and we need him to know that you're his pack now."

He nods slowly, still petting the dog. I can practically see the wheels turning behind his eyes. If I had to guess, he's asking himself if he's ready for this responsibility, if he's going to be able to take care of a dog when he can hardly take care of himself. "Part of the therapeutic element of having a service dog is that it helps most people form new routines. It pushes them to get out of bed every day, take a walk, stick to a meal plan. Sometimes it's not all that easy to function on your own, but when someone's counting on you, it can give you a reason to get better."

He doesn't say anything, but he looks marginally less worried about it. I think some part of him believes what I'm saying could be true, even if he doesn't have much trust in himself right now.

Since Ranger and Benny need a few minutes to get acquainted, I tell him I need to get Benny's things from the truck and take my time doing so.

It was a bittersweet feeling gathering up Benny's favorite toys this morning and portioning out a week's worth of food for him. I printed off his care instructions, which are laid out in an easy-to-understand format with strategic bullet points and a few pink highlights over parts I think are particularly important. It's always hard to let a dog go, but there's nothing quite like the joy of knowing how much they love having such an important job to do. A dog with a job is a happy dog.

By the time I make my way back over, holding a large cardboard box full of stuff, Ranger is kneeling on the ground, and Benny is slobbering all over his face. My heart swells at the sight of Ranger's genuine smile.

"Is this normal?" he asks. "I thought service dogs were supposed to be very serious and business-like."

I chuckle. "Therapy dogs are a little different, and he knows when to take his job seriously," I assure him. "But a big part of his job is becoming your best friend. Which, it looks like, is off to a great start."

He wipes his face off and gets to his feet. Now that he's fully facing me, his shirt still nowhere to be seen, I notice a metallic barbell through his left nipple. Cheese and crust, nipple piercings are my fracking kryptonite. I've never seen a nipple piercing I didn't want to bite, but dang it, I'm a professional. I manage to tear my eyes away from his chest and act like one.

"Why don't we go inside, and we can talk some more about Benny?" I turn around too fast in my excitement to tell him all about his new pooch's schedule. I didn't realize how close I was standing to one of the fence posts. With the box in my hands, I don't even see it before I'm stumbling over it, tossing Benny's things into the air.

Sassafras, falling on my ass hurts, and for a few seconds, I'm more focused on my bruised ego and the fact that dog toys and baggies of food are scattered around me than getting up.

Then I notice the shift in the air.

5

RANGER

One moment, everything is fine. The next, the darkness is coming at me. Nausea is fighting his way up, and my knees buckle from under me. Where am I? Back in the sandbox.

No, I'm not.

Where's Brooklyn? Where the fuck is he? Alex! I want to scream for him, but I can't.

Panic claws at me, and bitterness fills my mouth.

I'm on the ground. How did I get there? I dig my fingers in the dirt. Dirt, not sand. How? What?

Something wet touches my hand, nudging it gently. I reach out. Fur. Soft fur. A dog? Why is there a dog? Is it a stray from some village?

If he gets in the way, he might get hurt, so I grab him. He allows me to hug him, and then I hold on to him, his smell invading my nose. He's so fresh and soft, and he keeps licking my hand, my arm, my cheek. My fingers find purchase in his fur, and I cling to him, embracing him with all I have, like he's my lifeline. And then, I'm back.

I'm on the ground, Benny stretched out on top of me, his

face pressed against mine, and I'm squeezing him to my chest. He whines softly between licks and gentle nudges, and I breathe in deeply. What happened?

Oh god. Oh, fuck no. Please tell me I didn't have a...

Dammit all to hell and back. I had an episode in front of Julian. I close my eyes again. I can't face him now. Not after this. No one was supposed to see me like this. No one has. Not my parents, not my brother. No one. This is *my* pain, and I don't want anyone else to witness it.

Did he even stay? I hope he left, but I know deep down he hasn't. He wouldn't, not without being certain I'm okay. Don't ask me how I know that, even when the fog that inevitably follows an episode settles in my brain. I'm so goddamn tired of this. Though it feels as if this was a short one and nowhere near as bad as it could have been, thanks to Benny.

I bury my face in his fur, and he lets out a *whoof*. What am I gonna say to Julian? Sorry for being a freak? For acting like a madman? Do I assure him he shouldn't be scared, even though I have no way of knowing whether he has reason to or not? I've never been violent during an episode, but then again, I've never had one around other people. That's primarily because I simply haven't been around other people. Not since it got this bad.

I thought I'd beaten it. After Lucky visited me, a month after I'd come back from my last deployment, I'd been so ashamed of the state he'd found me in that I vowed to get my shit together. And for a month or two, three, that worked. I gained some weight, managed to get some stuff done, and I even joined him and his men on a sailing trip.

But then the package from Alex had come and, with it, the nightmares. The darkness. This deep sense of hopelessness I'd never thought I'd feel. I'm a fucking Army Ranger.

How did I turn into this? Shame and embarrassment fill me all over again.

I don't know how long I've been on the ground, pretending nothing happened, but it must've been more than a few minutes. Time to face the music, I guess. I open my eyes and reluctantly let go of Benny. He gets off me, but he's right by my side as I scramble to my feet with a complete lack of coordination.

Julian stands at a distance, watching me. Or us, I should say. His face shows concern, but not the disgust or shock I expected.

"Are you okay?" he asks. "Is there anything I can do?"

The pity in his eyes kills me. I've always been the kind of man others admired. Strong, a leader. A Ranger. And now? I'm a shell of my former self, a shadow of who I once was... and I have no idea how to deal with that.

"I need to sleep," I say, my voice raw.

"Okay. I can come back tomorrow. Would you like me to leave Benny here, or would you prefer some time alone?"

I blink. He'd be okay with leaving his dog with me, even after what just happened? "I'm not sure I can take care of him."

His face softens. "You don't need to. Allow him to take care of you. All he needs is food, and I've brought enough for a week. I've prepared written instructions, so it's super easy."

He points at the carton box he dropped when he tripped over the pole. Several bags of dog food, toys, and some other stuff I can't identify this quickly.

"I'm... I can't think right now."

"I understand. I'll put this on your kitchen counter and leave, and I'll call tomorrow."

I nod, too dazed to say anything. I don't want him here

with his bright blue eyes, which are supposed to be repulsed or scared or even shocked but instead show nothing but kindness.

Julian kneels. "Benny," he says. Benny licks my hand a last time, then darts over to Julian and immediately lies at his feet. Julian rubs Benny's head affectionately. "Such a good boy. You did good, Benny. You made me proud. Now, go take care of him, okay? This is what we trained for. You've got this."

The episode must have fucked me up more than I realized because a mushy feeling settles in my chest as I watch them. Benny happily wags his tail, his face showing joy and pride at the praise. Julian kisses his head, then rises.

"He's yours now," he tells me, and then he walks off with the box into the house. He comes out with empty hands, and with a last wave, he gets into his car and drives off.

Benny is at my side, tilting his head expectantly. He's mine now, Julian said. The weight of that responsibility lies like a heavy stone in the pit of my stomach. "I'll try." I scratch him behind his ears. "That's all I can promise you, but don't expect miracles from me."

He wags his tail again, his eyes fixed on me with a love and affection I don't deserve. "Let's get some sleep. I'm wiped."

He follows me obediently as I go inside and take a quick shower. He lies down in the corner of the bathroom, keeping watch, and when I crawl into bed, completely exhausted, he settles on the floor right next to my bed. I pat the bedding. "Come here, Benny."

He doesn't need to be told twice, and he snuggles right up to me. With my arm around him and his silky fur against my cheek, I fall asleep mercifully quick.

6

JULIAN

Ranger and Benny are on my mind the rest of the night. I can't believe I was so careless. I've been doing this work for vets with PTSD for years now, and early on, I messed up more than once before I finally decided I needed to do better. I did all the research I could on PTSD—reading articles, speaking with therapists who specialize in PTSD treatment, talking with veterans. I learned about being careful to respect a veteran's space, pay attention to triggers, and never move too quickly when they're not expecting it.

In many ways, I realized I need to treat them like I do my horses because that same part of their brain, the part that warns them danger could be around any corner, is always active. But even after all that effort, I still triggered him.

I was proud to see how quickly Benny responded, doing exactly what he'd been trained to do to comfort his new person and grounding him when he needed it. But I can't stop feeling terrible for causing him so much distress in the first place.

I've spent half the day trying to work up my courage to

give him a call so I can set up a time to go back over there and finish with his Benny orientation. Not courage because I'm afraid of him but courage because I feel like an ass.

Speaking of asses, Doc tugs my shirt between his teeth, then bumps me with his muzzle.

"Sorry, you're right. You deserve my full attention," I say and sign the apology, then continue to brush his soft coat. He's been rolling in the dirt, so a good brush was long overdue.

I have no doubt that Ranger can manage to take care of Benny, at least for a few days. But I do need to finish showing him the hand signals I've trained Benny with and check if he has any questions once he's had a chance to read through all the paperwork. I just haven't managed to decide if it's better I call now so he knows everything is okay, or if I should give him another couple of days.

The sound of tires crunching against my gravel driveway has me furrowing my eyebrows. I set down the brush and head out of the barn to see who might be here. Apparently, Doc is interested too, even if he's too deaf to have heard the car drive up, because he follows me out.

I recognize the truck from Ranger's driveway, and sure enough, the truck stops, and that's exactly who gets out. He lets Benny out while I hurry over.

"Is everything okay? Is there a problem with Benny?" The dog bounces over to me, looking perfectly fine and happy. Did he change his mind about keeping Benny? I can't imagine another reason he would've taken the time to search for my address and drive out here like this unannounced.

"Benny's great," he assures me, reaching down to pet the dog's head. "I wanted to stop by to apologize."

"Apologize?" Doc starts to chew on my clothes again.

"Stop," I say and sign to him. "Go back to the barn." The donkey does as I tell him, making a noise of protest before trotting back to the open barn.

I turn back to Ranger, who looks more confused than dejected, which is an improvement at least. "Does that donkey know sign language?"

I shrug. "He's deaf."

For some reason that doesn't seem to clear things up for him, but I don't know how else to explain it, so I focus back on the other issue. "If anyone needs to apologize, it's me."

He shakes his head, running his fingers through his hair and staring off into the distance. Whether he's watching my horses in the field or just avoiding my gaze, I can't tell. "I wasn't going to hurt you or anything. At least I don't think I was." He grimaces.

I have the urge to reach out and touch him, comfort him. But there's no fracking way I'm going to mess up with him again, so I keep my hands firmly to myself, even if it's physical torture for a hugger like me to resist squeezing every ounce of darkness out of him. I know it doesn't work that way, but it would be nice if it did.

"You really don't need to apologize. I'm sorry for triggering you. Since you're here, do you want to finish your orientation?"

By this point, the rest of the dogs have realized that things are happening, and all five of them descend on us. PP keeps her distance, eyeing Benny warily like she's concerned he's coming back after all. I pet her head reassuringly and shoo the other dogs away.

"That would be great," he agrees. "I managed to get out of bed last night to feed him dinner before crashing again. And I was up bright and early to make sure I could get him on a good feeding schedule and let him outside."

I smile at the hint of pride in his voice. He didn't think he could manage a dog, but it's already starting to set better habits for him, helping him build a daily routine.

"It sounds like you're doing a fantastic job so far. Let me show you some of the signals he knows. I have him trained for verbal commands as well as hand gestures, so you can use either or both."

"Do I need to learn sign language for him?" He glances toward the barn, where Doc is watching us like some creeptastic donkey stalker.

I scrunch my eyebrows and cock my head to one side. "Of course not. Benny can hear just fine."

A rusty-sounding laugh bursts from Ranger's lips, which seems to surprise him as much as it does me.

I spend the next half hour going over the signals and telling him all the little quirks of Benny's personality, like how he's happiest if he can have a clean sock to carry around at night and that sometimes he likes to put his dry kibble into his water bowl and then go bobbing for the pellets.

"Do you have any questions?" I ask once I'm sure I've covered everything. He's looking a little worried and uncertain again. And since I *still* can't hug him, I do the next best thing to ease his concerns. "The number you already have for me is my cell phone. You can text me anytime. I'd love to hear how...Benny is doing." I almost said how *he's* doing, but I hardly know the man, and he'll probably think I'm beyond weird for worrying about a perfect stranger.

That seems to soothe him some. "Thanks, I appreciate that." Silence falls between us, and Ranger turns his attention to the horses again.

"Do you want to see my farm? I can introduce you to everyone."

"Um…" He glances down at Benny, like he's hoping the dog will give him an excuse to beg off.

"There's a goat that hates me," I tempt with a grin, and he does that gravely laugh again.

"Sure, why not?"

I start with the barn, giving him a proper introduction to Doc this time. He pats the donkey's head cautiously, and Doc nuzzles his hand, then dips his head and butts it against Benny, who huffs indignantly.

I lead him out the back door and wave at the goat in the field with the horses. "This is Butler."

"Why does he have pink pool noodles on his horns?"

"Because he hates me," I explain again.

"Are you sure it's not the other way around?" he deadpans, and I bark out a laugh.

"Fair question. I'll have a chat with him about it. Maybe he'd prefer purple or blue," I concede, and I get another look from Ranger like he's sure I've lost my mind. I point out each of the horses, giving their names and telling him a little about each of them. "See that brown one with the white nose? That's Talon. He's in an *Avengers* movie that's coming out next year. He's had Chris Hemsworth's legs wrapped around him, which is more than I can say for myself, unfortunately."

As soon as the joke is out of my mouth, my face heats. Flapjacks, that was inappropriate. Ranger may be here on my farm, but this is still a business relationship. I glance over and find Ranger with a sad expression on his face that morphs into an attempt at a smile when he sees me looking.

"That's really cool about the movie." The words sound interested enough, but his tone is a little flat.

"Yeah…" Talk about awkward. "You like chickens?" I ask enthusiastically in hopes of changing the subject.

"I don't know any personally," he answers dryly, and when I realize it's a joke, I grin.

"Well, you're going to love these ladies," I assure him, showing him the chicken coop. "These lovely hens are Blanche, Dorothy, Sophia, and Rose."

"You named your chickens after the *Golden Girls*?" He quirks an eyebrow.

"Sure. Why? Do you think I should've gone with *The A-Team*?" I tap my chin. "They're female, but I doubt they'd mind much either way."

This time his laugh is slightly less tight, and a sense of accomplishment fills me. I look over at him and find a smile just barely emerging. It looks nice on him. I bet it would look even nicer if it was a full smile.

7

RANGER

That went about as well as I could have hoped for, so I'll chalk it up as a win. I'll take my victories where I can get them, since they're far and few between at the moment. Julian is, I have to admit, incredibly kind and understanding. I'm usually pretty good at picking up nonverbal signals, but his were completely congruent with his words. He wasn't lying, which makes me feel marginally better about having an episode in his presence.

It's still embarrassing as fuck, but there isn't much I can do about it now. At least he's not scared of me, as far as I can tell, though I'm not sure if that's smart or not. I've read some absolute horror stories about vets with PTSD who got violent, for example, with their partner.

Here's a tip: don't Google worst-case scenarios of whatever you have. Trust me on this. Fuck knows I did not need the extra stress of fearing I might get violent with someone as my condition progresses.

On the drive back, Benny has his head out the window, and the look of sheer ecstasy on his face makes me smile. I remember that from Maggie, one of our dogs when I was a kid. She loved nothing more than long drives with her head out the windows. The last thing my dad did for her when he had to get her to the vet to help her cross the rainbow bridge was to drive an extra few miles so she could enjoy it one last time.

And of course, it's classic me to think of that sad memory when I watch Benny because I seem to be a glass-half-empty guy these days. God, I would give anything to feel the optimism I used to have, the hope that tomorrow would be better. Though looking at Benny, it's hard not to feel that having him there will make things a little better.

When we get home, I work on practicing the hand signals with Benny like Julian showed me, and much to my delight, I get them right. I reward Benny with the dog treats Julian provided and make a mental note to stop by the store tomorrow to pick up more dog food for Benny. And maybe some toys?

I take a picture of Benny with my phone and send it to Lucky.

Ranger: meet Benny. He's mine now

Lucky: he looks so sweet

Ranger: he's a cuddlebug for sure

Lucky: is he allowed to sleep in your bed?

I frown. Julian never mentioned anything about that. Benny did sleep in my bed last night, but maybe that's not smart? I'd better check.

Ranger: This is Ranger

Ranger: Mack

Ranger: Mack Stone

Julian: I had your number saved, no worries. Would you like me to call you Ranger or Mack?

. . .

I LEAN BACK in my chair. That question is far more difficult to answer than it should be. I've gone by Ranger since I served my first tour abroad as an Army Ranger, fourteen years ago, and somehow managed to make an impossible kill shot. I earned that name, and I've proudly used it ever since. No one calls me Mack except my parents and, on occasion, Lucky.

But somehow, it feels like I've lost the right to my nickname. How long can I cling to the fame of the past? Because that's what it feels like. Still, everything in me rebels at calling myself Mack.

Ranger: Ranger, please

Julian: Okay, Ranger it is. What can I do for you?

Ranger: is Benny allowed to sleep in my bed?

Julian: I don't know. Is he?

I stare at his reply for a while.

Ranger: is that your way of saying it's my call?

Julian: Yes. He's your dog. You set the rules.

Ranger: I wasn't sure if it would set a wrong example. I don't know. Like, distract him? Or something.

Julian: If having him in your bed makes you feel better, then that's where he should be. Allow him to do his job and comfort you. You can't spoil him with things like that, honestly.

Ranger: okay, thanks. Sorry for disturbing you.

Julian: No problem at all. You can text me anytime you have a question. I'm always happy to help.

WOW, he really is chipper. What's funny is that it's not even annoying, since I somehow sense it's his natural disposition. He's Happy, and I'm Grumpy, and the fact that I'm using a fucking Disney movie as a reference is reason enough to make me even more depressed. Except it's kinda funny, and I grin at Benny, who stares back with a goofy smile, his tail wagging.

"Maybe he should've called you Happy," I tell him. "Because you certainly look the part."

Benny's response is increased wagging, so I interpret that as him thinking I'm funny. I'm not, but he doesn't need to know that.

Ranger: yes, he can. I make the rules.

Lucky: Let me guess. You just checked that with the dog trainer?

My brother is way too perceptive. Fucking parole officer, always reading even the most subtle signals.

Ranger: fuck you

Lucky: nah, thanks. I've got my hands full with my two men already. No need to add brocest

Ranger: oh god, that's... fuck off

BUT I DO smile as I put my phone away. Benny nudges my hand, and I spend a good two minutes petting him, which is strangely calming. "How about we head to the store now? We could get some more toys for you. Julian said to keep you engaged with different kinds of challenges, so we could see if they have something fun for you?"

I didn't know dogs could give a "duh" look, but Benny just did as if I asked him the most stupid question ever, and maybe I did. Another car ride must sound like fun to him. I put on his special harness Julian told me to make him wear whenever we're in public so he'd be recognized as a service dog.

We make it to the store, where it's blissfully quiet. Good. I don't like people. I wasn't a massive fan before I was diagnosed, and now even less. Benny obediently walks right by my side as we cruise the aisles, looking for the pet stuff. I've never had reason to locate it, so it takes me a while to find the right aisle.

"Excuse me."

I whirl around at the stern male voice, my heart rate jumping into overdrive as I immediately break out in a sweat. Fuck, fuck, fuck.

"You can't bring a dog into this store."

My vision blurs, fog descending, but then Benny licks my hand, and it breaks the pattern. I take a deep breath and rest my hand on his head, holding on to him like an anchor. "He's a service dog," I say between gritted teeth.

The store employee crosses his arms, frowning. "You're not blind."

No shit, Sherlock. "You don't have to be blind to have a service dog."

His frown is anything but friendly. "Look, dude, you don't look like you have any handicaps, so why the fuck would you need a service dog? Seems to me you got that vest somewhere online just so you could bring your dog in."

"Paul, do we have a problem here?"

An older man in his seventies joins us. I've seen him in town several times, though I have no idea who he is. His eyes are sharp, and his face is stern as he addresses the store employee.

"I was just telling this gentleman his dog needs to leave, Mr. Sherman."

"Why?"

"He doesn't look like he needs a service animal, so I'm pretty sure he's faking it."

Everything in me is screaming to get the fuck out, but at this point, I'm not even sure my legs would support me. With all my willpower, I hold on to Benny, who leans against me, solid as a rock, giving me the support I need. Literally and figuratively.

Mr. Sherman's jaw tightens, and his eyes are blazing. "Do you know who this is?" he snaps at Paul, jerking his head at me.

Who I am? What is he talking about? Does he have me confused with someone else?

"Uh, no?" Paul shoots me another look, more hesitant now.

"This is Mack Stone, a distinguished veteran of the United States Army Rangers. He's the recipient of a bronze and a silver star and served his country with honor."

I move my head up. How does he know? Tears spring in my eyes. Hearing this man list my name with so much respect in his voice does more to me than any well-meaning "thank you for your service," and I have to swallow away the tightness in my throat.

"I would hope that this store would treat decorated veterans with more dignity and respect than you're showing right now, Paul."

Mr. Sherman's words are ice stabs now, and Paul has become several degrees paler, which is strangely satisfying. "I had no idea, Mr. Sherman. I—"

"Don't apologize to me. Apologize to him."

Paul turns toward me, his face void of the derision it showed earlier. "I do apologize, Mr. Stone. I wasn't aware of your service, and I... I apologize."

He all but runs off, and a deep sigh of relief falls from my lips, and my shoulders lose some of the tension.

"Take a few minutes to collect yourself. I'll wait until you feel ready again," Mr. Sherman says, his voice much warmer now.

How does he know what I'm going through? Because he *knows*. There's no doubt in my mind, not based on how he looks at me, the kind compassion in his eyes, and the information he spouted about me. Somehow, he knows me, even though I have no clue who he is.

But I can't deal with that right now. He's right. I do need a minute, and I sink to my knees and hug Benny with all my might, burying my face in his fur. He whines and presses his wet nose against my neck, grounding me.

When I sense I'm steady enough—which has to be at least five minutes later--I rise again but keep my hand on Benny's head. I still need that connection. Mr. Sherman is still there, standing guard.

"Thank you," I finally manage.

"Paul is not the sharpest tool. Not that you should have to explain or defend yourself to anyone."

"I'm sorry, but have we met before? My memory is not the best."

His smile is almost grandfatherly. "Only on paper. You bought my house. I lived there for almost fifty years with my wife, Doris."

Fifty years. Wow. That's a long time to be with someone. I can't even imagine. "Oh, okay."

"I did a little digging when you put an offer in. I wanted to know who bought it, since that place was and is special to me. I know I let the house go, but after Doris died, I... I lacked the energy and will to put any effort into it."

"I'm not sure I'm faring much better," I admit. "I had big plans, but I haven't accomplished much yet."

"That's okay. You'll get there. Grieving takes time."

It does, but how does he know I'm grieving?

"I served in Vietnam. I know war trauma and grieving when I see it."

He extends his hand slowly enough I see it coming. Then he grabs my shoulder for a firm squeeze. "One day at a time, Ranger. You'll get there. Rangers lead the way, right?"

I nod, too stunned to even say anything.

"Take care, Ranger. I'm sure we'll meet again."

It's only when I'm halfway back to my house that I realize I still didn't get Benny his treats and toys, and that while he deserves them now more than ever. "We'll get them tomorrow," I promise him, and Benny just sends me a goofy smile, then turns his attention back to the open window.

8

JULIAN

"Cut," the director calls, and I give Daisy, my black mare, the signal to stand still, then step onto the set to offer her a carrot.

The actor isn't quite as cooperative as my horse, because he hops down and makes his displeasure with the director known in an obnoxious fashion. Not my circus, not my monkeys, so I just pet Daisy's nose while they work out their dispute.

While I wait, I reach into my pocket to check my phone. I felt it vibrate a little while ago while we were in the middle of the scene. A smile jumps to my lips as soon as I see that it's a text from Ranger.

"It doesn't mean anything," I whisper to Daisy. "He's still adjusting to having a dog, so it's natural he'll have a lot of questions."

And a lot of questions he has had indeed. In the past week, I've gotten no fewer than five or six texts each day, asking me which food is best for Benny and if there's any validity to the whole raw diet thing. He even sent me several pictures of Benny's poop, asking if it looks normal. Should he be brushing the dog's teeth... It's cute, if I'm being honest. I mean, not *cute*, but sweet...okay, fine, cute too.

Today's text is a picture of Benny gently carrying around what appears to be a stuffed turkey.

Julian: So cute!

Ranger: It seems like having something to hold soothes him. And if he's meant to be comforting me, I figure he should be as calm as possible.

I chuckle at the comment.

Julian: Great point. Retrievers are always calmest when they have something to hold in their mouths. The turkey was an interesting choice.

Ranger: I gave him a few options, and that seemed to be his preference. I got a few others for him in case he has a change of heart later, though.

I LAUGH AGAIN, my heart warming at how quickly he seems to have bonded with Benny, and it's obvious how much good the dog is doing for him. It's a small thing, but I notice in the background of the picture, his house looks slightly tidier than when I was there before.

I've volunteered a lot of energy and time, not to mention money, into working for the Pups for Patriots program, and I've never seen this side of the process firsthand. I've always had to believe in what I had learned about the benefits and trust in my dogs, but to actually witness Ranger's slow improvement with my own two eyes is magical.

Ranger: What are you up to today?

THE QUESTION SURPRISES ME. Yes, we've texted very regularly for the past week but *never* about anything except Benny. Is there some line I shouldn't cross here? The program is free to vets, so he's not technically a paying client or anything, which means fraternization shouldn't be an issue. He probably needs a friend, and let's face it, I'm not exactly swimming in companionship either...well, the two-legged nonfurry kind of companionship anyway. Although I'm also not opposed to the right amount of body hair.

My mind wanders back to the day I brought Benny to Ranger, specifically the shirtless part. The part *before* I tripped and made an ass of myself by setting off his PTSD. My body gets a little tingly as I remember the tuft of dark hair surrounding his belly button and trailing down to the waistband of his jeans. And that silver nipple stud.

Before I can spend too much time shamelessly drooling over the mental image of a half-naked Ranger that I've conjured up, the actor strides back over to Daisy in an angry huff. I put a hand up and stop him before he can mount her again.

"You need to cool your energy off," I say, moving between him and the horse.

He snorts and rolls his eyes. "It's a horse, and I want to get this damn scene wrapped already. I have dinner plans."

"I don't care what kind of plans you have. Horses are sensitive to energy, and if you come at her the way you are, she's not going to be as receptive to my signals. It's dangerous."

He grits his teeth, darting his eyes between me and Daisy, like he's wondering if he can get around me to get back in the saddle. He's dreaming if he thinks I'll let that happen. I may not be the biggest guy in the world, but if there's one thing I've learned in all my time taming giant beasts, it's that energy is everything. I square my shoulders and fix him with an "I will not be fucked with" look, and just like the bear—animal bear, not human bear, just FYI—I once tried that on, he turns around and stalks off, muttering under his breath. To be clear, the bear didn't mutter, but it did make some annoyed grumbling noises.

While I wait for him to adjust his attitude, I return to my text exchange with Ranger. I was too lost in my drool-worthy musings to respond before.

Julian: Taming horses and grouchy actors. You?

THE MESSAGE IS MARKED as read, and little bubbles pop up, then disappear, then pop up again. I don't get to find out what he's taking so much time to say, though, because grouchy actor, Ryan, returns with much more appropriate energy this time. I step out of the way and pat Daisy's nose while he clambers onto her back.

After another few hours, the scene is finally wrapped, and I load my horse back up into her trailer. I hop into the cab of my truck, pull out my phone again to see the message I missed from Ranger.

Ranger: Wow, that's...impressive. You must think I'm a joke, not even able to handle regular day-to-day shit while you're out there making movies and training animals and fuck knows what else.

My heart gives a sad pang for him.

Julian: Pretty sure if I were in a combat situation, I'd soil myself on the spot and then run the other way, screaming like a child. You're not giving yourself nearly enough credit.

Ranger: yeah...

I FROWN AT HIS RESPONSE, setting my phone in the cup holder and putting the truck into gear to get us home. While

I drive, I think about how it must feel to go from seeing yourself as this badass, capable soldier to looking in the mirror every day at someone who's struggling to do the simplest things. Forget the fact that a heck of a lot of trauma went into the transformation; it must be difficult to reconcile those two different versions.

When I get back to the farm, I unload Daisy and do a quick check of the barn to make sure everyone has fresh water, then head inside. In the last week, Rita and Calzone have been placed in a new home as well, and only three dogs greet me, which is a woefully low number of dogs if you ask me.

I give PP a kiss on the snout and pat Theodore and Lila on the head. I'll probably have them placed within the next few weeks if I had to guess, which will mean a new batch of puppies, a stage I always look forward to and dread at the same time.

I kick off my shoes, stroll into the living room, and flop down onto the couch. I pull out my phone again and stare at the recent text exchange with Ranger, an unsettled feeling in my chest at his perception of himself. I'm not a therapist, and I know that, but giving him Benny was the best thing I could offer him, but maybe friendship wouldn't hurt either?

Julian: I'm trying to decide between watching a Hallmark movie or a Lifetime movie. The struggle is real.

Ranger: is there a difference?

Julian: Is there a difference?! Holy potatoes, I cannot believe you just asked that.

Ranger: Holy potatoes?

Julian: Don't change the subject. I'm about to school you here, and you need to pay attention...

. . .

Ranger's education on the difference between Hallmark and Lifetime segues into a discussion about our favorite and, more importantly, least favorite movies that lasts most of the night, meaning that I never get around to watching a movie after all, which is perfectly fine with me. Our conversation is far more interesting than what either Hallmark or Lifetime has to offer.

As I climb into bed, one last text comes through: a selfie of Ranger and Benny snuggling in bed, and dammit, the man is shirtless again. If we're going to become friends, he's going to need to learn to stay fully clothed at all times.

Julian: Cute. Sleep tight.

I set my phone on my nightstand, and PP jumps up into bed next to me. I sigh and run my fingers through her fur. I'm not lonely; I have Princess Pinecone. Not lonely at all.

9

RANGER

I don't know how it happened, but sometime in the last two weeks, Julian and I have become friends. I mean, I'm no expert on friendships. Being in the Army makes it hard to maintain them, but I'm pretty sure texting every day suggests more than casual acquaintances.

And we're not talking one or two texts either. The messages fly back and forth throughout the day, and I'm even sending him pics. Including selfies. My god, Lucky would have a fucking heart attack if he knew.

I don't do selfies. They're silly and stupid and egocentric, and I always feel like a complete moron when I try to take one. And yet here we are, and the selfies game is on point, as Julian stated.

By the way, people post YouTube videos on how to take a good selfie. Who knew? There's a search term I never thought I'd use. I have to admit that watching those videos did improve my pics significantly. It turns out that the angle can be the difference between looking like Jacob Marley brought back to life or an actual living person. Go me. The fact that I shaved helped as well.

Julian's pics are way better than mine, of course. Way cuter too. He always has this sparkle in his eyes as if he always has a reason to laugh.

It's close to midnight, and I'm already in bed, trying to get to that point where I'm so tired I fall asleep instantly, but I find myself staring at his latest picture for minutes. It's a selfie of him and his gorgeous husky, who looked annoyed at the indignity of having to pose. Can't say I blame her.

Something about him draws me in. He's so...alive. So vibrant and energetic. In a way, he's what I want to be again. At least, that's what I tell myself as I open my messages again to look at other pictures. I'm attracted to his energy, his carefree and happy spirit.

As a friend. Attracted as a friend, let's make that crystal clear. Not in any other way. The waters of my sexual identity are muddy enough without adding more confusion to the mix. I can't be attracted to him as more than friends because that would be...

I don't even wanna go there. Just the thought sends a stab of pain through my heart so fierce it takes my breath away. No one will ever be able to take Alex's place, even if we were never more than friends. Brothers in arms.

Julian reminds me of Alex in a way. Alex was much cockier, with a shit-eating grin that made me trust him and believe in whatever cockamamy plan he'd come up with. He only had to smile, and I was ready to follow him to the ends of the earth.

Julian is less arrogant, less cocksure, though he's no pushover. He's got a backbone, and I like that. He's built a thriving business, which he should be proud of. But he also exudes that zest for life Alex had as well, that *joie de vivre,* as the French call it so eloquently. That's what attracts me to them, and there's nothing wrong with that. In fact, I'd argue that building friendships is healthy and definitely progress for me.

"Don't you agree, Benny?" I ask my new very best friend, who hasn't left my side yet. I never expected one dog to make such a difference, but he has.

Benny lifts his head, his tongue lolling as he pants. I frown. He's been lying next to me for the past half hour. Why the hell is he panting?

"You okay, buddy?"

I rest my hand on his head. Does he feel clammy? Like he has a fever? I have no idea. Do dogs even get a fever? I swipe away Julian's pic and do a quick Google search. Hmm, dogs can get a fever, and if they do, it's usually a sign of infection. I check the list of symptoms that could indicate he has a fever.

Are his eyes red? Not really, but it's hard to see in the faint light of my bedside lamp. Okay, warm ears, then. I rub his ears, which certainly feel warm to me. I lay my hand on my bare chest to compare. Yup, they're definitely warmer than my skin. My belly tightens. Is something wrong with him? His nose feels a little dry as well, and when I stroke his head again, he whimpers. Is he in pain?

I'm calling Julian's number before I even realize what time it is, but much to my surprise, he picks up fast. "Ranger, you okay?" he asks, sounding sleepy.

"It's Benny."

I hear rustling. "What's wrong with him?" Julian's voice is loaded with worry.

"He's panting, and I think he has a fever. I'm not sure, but—"

"Try to let him drink water. I'm on my way."

He ends the call, and a wave of relief flows through me. "I'm gonna unlock the front door for Julian, and then I'll be right back, okay?" I tell Benny. His response is more panting. What the hell is wrong with him?

I hurry toward the door, then grab Benny's water bowl and rush back to the bedroom. I don't give a flying fuck if my bed gets a little wet. It would be the most action this mattress has seen in a long time, I can assure you.

"Want some water?"

Benny obediently laps up some water, but then he lays his head on his paws again. I just hold him close, my worry growing as the panting continues, and I count the minutes until the front door opens.

"Ranger?" Julian calls out.

"I'm in my bedroom!"

Julian comes all but running into my room and screeches to a halt. His jaw drops, and his gaze flickers to my... Oops, I'm wearing nothing else but my tight, black boxer briefs. Well, he's going to have to deal with it. I have more important things to worry about than getting dressed.

He visibly swallows, then looks away as he clears his throat. "Right, let's have a look at Benny. Hey, boy, what's happening?"

Benny, who got up from the bed as soon as Julian walked in, licks Julian's outstretched hand, his tail wagging furiously. "He's not lethargic," Julian says as he runs his hands over Benny's face, then his ears.

As if to prove Julian's point, Benny lets out an excited bark. I scratch my head. "He's been panting the whole time."

"Hmm. I wonder why."

He keeps petting Benny, and my stomach clenches as I watch him. Did I do something wrong? Did I somehow harm Benny?

Then Julian gasps and starts laughing, a snort-giggle

that transforms into a full-out laugh. What the hell is happening?

"Holy beans," Julian says, wiping his eyes. Benny barks, clearly as confused about the laughter as me. "I can't even... This is... Gosh, how do I explain this?"

I straighten my shoulders and cross my arms. "Give it your best try."

10

JULIAN

I'm a huge proponent of neutering, but since the foundation primarily works with large breed dogs who are prone to orthopedic problems if neutered too young, we usually give the new owner a certificate for free neuter at their local vet. The certificate was in Ranger's packet, but I must've forgotten to discuss it with him. Now, none of this would normally be a big problem, but when I got out of my truck to come into the house, I heard coyote howls not too far off, and if I had to guess...

"He's, well, he's horny," I bite the bullet and explain.

Ranger's eyes drop to Benny's penis and go wide, his cheeks blushing pink. It's totally not adorable to see a big, tough army ranger blush. Nope, not doing a thing for me. On another note, denial is not just a river in Egypt.

"Horny?" He coughs. "Um, okay, one more weird question, but is his...uh...his penis supposed to look like that?" Ranger gestures vaguely, and I can't decide if I want to laugh or dig a hole to bury myself in. I've never been particularly shy about sex, but having to explain a dog's erection to a ridiculously attractive, mostly naked man...in his bedroom...in the middle of the night...yeah, this is a little much. It definitely doesn't help that I may or may not have been having a semiracy dream about said mostly naked man right around the time my phone rang.

"It's normal," I assure him. "That's his knot, and, uh, yeah, we're going to give Benny some privacy and stop staring at his dick." I encourage the dog to put his leg down to protect his virtue.

I turn away from the bed and bump right into Ranger and his miles and miles of bare skin. He chuckles, putting his hands on my shoulders to steady me before I can topple backward or otherwise make an ass of myself...again.

"Thanks." I smile and take a step back to put a little space between us. My eyes, acting entirely of their own volition, drop to the front of his *very* tight boxer briefs. *Bojangles, that is a big bulge.* "I should...uh...yup," I stammer like an idiot, closing my traitorous eyes and thumbing blindly in the direction of the door.

"Wait." His fingers wrap around my forearm, and my breath catches while my cock perks up at the touch. "I'm sorry I got you out of bed in the middle of the night."

"It's no big deal. I couldn't sleep anyway," I lie, opening my eyes but keeping them trained on his face with great effort. Are his eyes always so sleepy-sexy?

"Do you maybe want to stay for a little while?" Ranger asks, and I fight back the hysterical excitement that rises in my chest. I dart a glance at the bed, then back at the man standing *way* too close and not close enough.

He doesn't mean stay to fool around. Of course he doesn't. We're friends, and he was worried about Benny. Now he feels bad that he made me drive out here. That's all.

"I have some hot cocoa powder. It's nothing fancy but..." he offers with a shrug. The sweet vulnerability in his expression is worse than kryptonite. I couldn't turn him down if my life depended on it.

"Sure, I'll stay for a little while," I agree.

Ranger hits me with a smile that nearly has me weak in the knees before he takes a step back and gestures toward the bedroom door. Right, of course. We can't make hot cocoa in his bedroom. Apparently, he has no intention of putting pants on as he steers me toward the kitchen without any stops. Cool, cool, cool. This is totally fine.

The kitchen looks slightly cleaner than it did the last time I was here. Grime still stains the grout, and the table is a bit sticky, but the dishes that were in the sink before are clean and in the drying rack. Baby steps.

I've lied to myself enough for one night, so I'm not even going to pretend my eyes don't linger on Ranger's mighty fine, tight butt as he makes himself busy heating milk and mixing in the cocoa powder. I breathe a sigh of relief when he sets a mug in front of me and then takes a seat, removing his glorious glutes from my eyeline. Not that the alluring view of his pierced nipples is much better.

"Sorry again about getting you out here in the middle of the night for nothing," he says, running his thumb absently over the handle of his mug and licking his lips.

"Oh, please." I wave my hand dismissively. "It wasn't for nothing. We have cocoa." I lift my mug and then take a sip. The hot liquid burns my tongue and down my throat as I swallow, but it tastes pleasantly chocolaty, so I'm not complaining.

"Please tell me this isn't the dumbest call from a worried owner you've had before?"

I laugh, then take another sip and relax in my seat. "Before I got into training and everything, I was a receptionist at a veterinary clinic, and we had some *interesting* clients."

"Oh yeah?" His eyes sparkle as he leans forward. The move seems unconscious, but I can't be sure. All I know is that I find myself leaning a bit closer too.

"There was this lady once who decided to breed her dogs." I roll my eyes to give him a hint about where this story is going. Ranger's foot bumps against mine under the table, sending little sparks all along my body, a charged energy seeming to crackle between us. "And I guess she just figured nature would take its course and that she wouldn't need to research anything."

"Uh-oh," he says with a grin.

"Yeah, uh-oh," I agree. "So I get this call one afternoon, and she's frantic because her dogs are stuck together." I pause for effect, waiting for his eyes to go wide with understanding.

"The knot?" he guesses, and I snort a laugh and nod.

"Yup, they were knotted. She told me she'd been throwing hot dogs at them for twenty minutes and couldn't get them to separate."

Ranger howls with laughter, and I join him.

"Oh my god, imagine being balls deep, and some crazy lady comes along chucking food at you," he cackles between bouts of laughter, causing us both to laugh even harder. He wipes away the tears streaming over his cheeks. I've never seen him so joyful and free.

"I don't know. I've been fucked by a few guys where the experience could've been *vastly* improved by snacks," I joke.

His laughter dies off, and it takes me a few seconds to notice an undercurrent of heat in his eyes. I lick my lips, and Ranger's eyes drop to my mouth, following the motion. My heart beats a little faster, and...I'm not sure if he's leaning in or I am, but between one blink and the next, our lips are pressed together.

My mind short-circuits as Ranger's hot and soft lips part against mine. He drags his tongue along the seam of my mouth, the taste of chocolate lingering.

But as quickly and unexpectedly as the lovely mouth-to-mouth started, it ends. He gasps and pulls back, leaving me suspended in space with the ghost of his kiss on my lips and a sick, guilty feeling in the pit of my stomach.

"I'd better go." I jump up so fast I nearly knock the chair over. Ranger tenses. I curse myself for my careless movements. Out of the corner of my eye, I see his fists clench, his chest rising slowly as he draws in a deep breath. "Sorry," I mutter, then flee from the kitchen and out the front door.

Once I'm in my truck, I turn the music up loud enough I won't be able to hear myself think, and I hightail it home.

11

RANGER

Fuck, fuck, fuck. What did I do? Did I do it? Or was it Julian? I can't even remember anymore how it happened. One second I was laughing, and the next, we were kissing. His lips were so soft, and he tasted so good, and I'm the biggest motherfucking asshole on the planet.

How could I do this to him? To myself? And most of all, to Alex?

I bury my head in my hands and groan out loud. Benny is immediately by my side and presses against my leg. "I fucked up big-time," I mumble, but he doesn't seem impressed.

How can I claim I loved Alex, that I still love him, and kiss another man? Isn't that an insult to the depth of my love for him? He was my...my light, my everything. The fact that I was too stupid to realize it until it was too late doesn't change that. He had my heart, and when he died, a part of me died with him.

Then how come I feel so alive when I'm with Julian? He has this aura of happiness, a joy of life, about him that makes me feel...different. Happier. Energetic. It's wrong, I know, but I can't seem to stay away from him. My darkness seeks the light inside him, maybe in a desperate attempt to chase some of the shadows away.

It also confirms that I'm really, really bisexual. After Alex, I thought that it had been a case of falling for him specifically. Loving someone for who they are rather than for their gender.

Gay for you, some people might've called it, though I think that's a strange term. Clearly, I'm not gay, considering I've had plenty of hookups with women. Satisfying ones, I might add. Unlike Lucky, who's always been one hundred percent gay. He may have waited with coming out, but there was never any doubt for him as to who he was attracted to.

For me, it could have been women and just Alex. Except it's not, and I don't know how to feel about that. I'm sick to my stomach for kissing Julian. That should've never happened. He couldn't be interested in me, and the idea I surprised him, that he may have kissed me back just because he felt sorry for me... It makes me even angrier with myself.

What a clusterfuck. And what's even worse is that the one person I want to talk to about this is Julian himself...and he couldn't understand because I've never told him about Alex. Hell, does Julian even know that I'm...not straight? He sure as fuck knows now, and I groan all over again.

Benny puts his head on my thigh, and I pet him. "Your horny episode fucked me over good, buddy. Thanks for that."

Benny wags his tail, grinning at me. I can't help but smile at him. "Let's try and get some sleep, you big goofball."

Benny is out like a light, but sleep won't come for me. I toss and turn, my mind spinning in endless circles of self-doubt, anger, blame, and right back to doubt again. I'm really being constructive. Not. I see every hour on the clock until it's past six in the morning...late enough to call the one person who could understand.

I'll never understand why Lucky doesn't get tired of me, but he answers immediately. "You okay?" are his first words.

I close my eyes. "No. I need to talk to you."

"Okay. I'll be there in two hours."

"You don't need to—"

"You're not driving, bro. Not in the state you're in. Take a hot shower, do some of that goddamn yoga you love so much, and I'll be there as soon as I can."

"Your work..." I protest weakly, even though everything inside me lights up with love and warmth for my brother.

"Can wait. I'll take the day off. Emergency family situation." Lucky uses that tone that makes clear the discussion is over.

"Okay," I capitulate. "I'll see you in a bit."

I do as he told me and take a shower, which makes me feel marginally better. Then I do a slow yoga routine focused on breathing, which always helps me center myself and push my stress levels down. Breakfast is oatmeal, which I don't like, but it's supposedly healthy, so whatever. Trust me, after eating in chow halls and forcing down MREs for so many years, oatmeal is nectar of the gods. Pure ambrosia.

I'm outside in the garden pulling weeds when Lucky's truck pulls up. Benny barks, and I give him the signal to quiet down. "Friend," I tell him. "He's a friend."

My best friend, in fact, and my throat closes up again. Fucking emotional sap that I am.

Lucky approaches me with care, as always reading my body language, but when I hold out my arms, he rushes over and hugs me tightly. "You don't have to talk," he says when he lets go of me. "I'm grateful you called and asked me to come. That's enough."

"Technically, I didn't ask you to come. You told me you would."

Lucky grins. "Technicality. Let's just say you wanted to ask me, but I already read your mind."

"Sure, we'll go with that," I say dryly.

I grab us both some cold waters from the fridge, and then we sit outside in the backyard in the shade. Benny finds a cool spot under the picnic table, one of the few areas that still has grass. The unrelenting sun has already reduced the once green grass to brown remnants. Summer in California, man.

Lucky is quiet, sipping his water and not even studying me. He's always been good at that, reading people and knowing when to give them space.

"I kissed another man," I finally say, and much to his credit, Lucky's only reaction is a quirk of his eyebrows and his hand holding the bottle still for a moment. Then he resumes drinking, his face under control again.

"Okay. Was it a good kiss?"

What a classic Lucky question. No judgment. Ever. "Yeah, though a little too brief to really determine the quality."

"What happened?"

That's the question, isn't it? What the fuck happened? Not merely with Julian and me, but with me in general. How did I become this person? How did everything change in one instant?

"His name was Alex," I say, and my throat tightens. "Not the man I kissed last night, but the other one... The one I fell in love with."

Lucky captures my hand and holds it as I gather the courage to tell him about the love I lost.

"He was in my unit. He was from New York and had the thickest New York accent you've ever heard. We all called him Brooklyn. Alex was... he was funny and quick-witted, with a sharp mind and an endless supply of jokes. He made us all laugh in tense moments, and we were better for it."

The memories make me smile. I can picture him so easily with that big grin on his face, the mischief dancing in his eyes. Pranks were his hobby, and he pulled so many stunts that in the end, no one ever believed a goddamn word out of his mouth anymore.

"He was gay. We'd served for over four years together when he told me one night, making me swear not to tell anyone else. I didn't. He felt safe with me, I guess, because I'd told him about you and about how proud I was of my brother...who also happened to be gay."

"That's a huge compliment and a testament to how much he trusted you, that he felt safe enough to share that," Lucky says softly.

"H-he was in love with me." My voice breaks. "I was too fucking stupid to realize it...or to understand that what I had started to feel for him was way more than friendship. I thought we were just close friends, a special friendship unlike I'd ever had with anyone else...but I was in love with him too. And I never got the chance to tell him."

Lucky gently squeezes my hand. "What happened to him?"

I swallow, but the tightness in my throat won't go away. "Our unit got attacked. We were doing a recon mission, but we had bad intel. The army camp that was supposed to only have a skeleton crew turned out to host at least three full platoons armed to the teeth. We walked straight into a trap.

Alex was hit by the first sniper bullet. Clean shot to his back, straight through his heart. He was dead on impact."

"Oh, Mack..." Lucky says, his voice choked up. "I'm so sorry."

"When I held his body, that's when I knew...but it was too late."

We sit for a long time, Lucky's quiet presence soothing the raw edges of my grief. It's strange, but I'm glad he knows now. It somehow makes it real, like I didn't just imagine my feelings for Alex.

"A couple of months after I had returned stateside, I received a package from his mother. He'd written me a just-in-case letter...a letter where he expressed his love for me and left me some of his personal things."

"The Yankees baseball cap," Lucky says, and I nod. "I wondered why you had switched allegiance, but that explains it."

"I can't help but deeply regret I never got to tell him... I feel so stupid that I didn't realize it in time. If I had..."

"Nothing would've come from it," Lucky says calmly. "You were in his chain of command. The intense friendship you had was already skirting the line. One of you would've had to transfer. We both know the army doesn't fuck around when it comes to relationships within a unit. Fraternization within the ranks would've gotten you court-martialed."

His words hit me like a dagger to the chest. In my head, I had pictured Alex and me together, serving proudly, but that would've never happened. The army would've never allowed me to be involved with him. I knew this, of course I did, but I guess I didn't allow that reality to pierce through my dreams of what could have been so far.

I sigh. "You're right, but still. It's hard not to look back and blame myself or wonder what if..."

"Yeah, I can imagine."

Somehow, telling Lucky about Alex makes the guilt a little lighter, the darkness inside me a little less oppressive.

"So who did you kiss last night?" Lucky finally asks.

"Julian. The dog trainer who trained Benny." I give Lucky the abbreviated version of my friendship with Julian. "I'm completely fucked up about this. It's too much, too soon."

"It's a kiss."

"I know, but... It feels like much more."

"I can understand that, but here's the thing. I agree you're not ready for a relationship. That's too much right now. So why not have some fun with him and explore that side of yourself? Just see where it takes you? Not everything has to be super serious from the get-go."

Huh. I never considered that as an option. To me, acknowledging my attraction to Julian meant somehow trying to start a new relationship. But I could opt to keep things light and just have fun. God knows I've always managed to keep it simple with women, so why not with him?

I just hope he still wants to talk to me after what happened.

12

JULIAN

P noses my hand, licking my fingers and pulling me from my third bout of daydreaming of the morning. It was the shortest kiss in history, and yet I've managed to think about it on a constant loop in my head for the last thirtysome hours.

No matter from what angle I look at it, I still haven't pinned down who made the first move. I'm terrified it was me. A friend in need calls me in the middle of the night because he's worried about his dog, and I respond by kissing him. Brilliant. Truly one of my best moments.

I scoff at myself and shake my head, tossing handfuls of chicken feed onto the ground for the girls to eat.

I've lost count of the number of times I've picked up my phone to call or text Ranger after getting home from his place two nights ago, but so far, the best thing I've come up with is "sorry I attacked you with my face," which seems woefully inadequate and probably not the best way to save our budding friendship.

The sound of a car pulling into the driveway has my

heart rate speeding up. No one ever comes out here, no one except Ranger. Well, he came *once*, but that feels like enough precedence for the hope fluttering in my stomach as I put the chicken feed away and walk briskly through the barn.

By the time I reach the other end, emerging where the driveway winds in front of the house, I've constructed a childish fantasy that Ranger is here to proclaim his undying love for me and that we'll live happily ever after. This is what happens when you're raised on too many Disney movies.

My heart lodges itself in my throat when I see him standing with his back to me, facing the house with tense shoulders, Benny glued to his side, wagging his tail slowly. PP grumbles at the sight of them, and I can't help but chuckle at her less than welcoming attitude.

Ranger spins around and raises a hand in a tentative wave when he sees me, and I do the same. Pathetic much?

"If I do anything stupid like try to kiss him again, do me a favor and bite me," I instruct Princess Pinecone. She sneezes, which I'm certain is a legally binding agreement.

Ranger and Benny make their way over.

"Hey," he says when they reach us, then grimaces. I can almost hear him mentally berating himself for the lame greeting, and I bite back a sympathetic grin.

"Hey," I echo, just to make him feel a little better. We stare at each other for a few heartbeats that seem to last the length of an entire millennium before I point my thumb at the barn.

"Want to pet Doc?" I offer because nothing fixes an awkward moment like a fluffy, deaf donkey.

He arches an eyebrow, then nods and follows me into the barn.

Doc is out grazing, so I guide Ranger through the stall and out the open door leading to his pasture. Butler decided to join him today instead of being with the horses, and he glares at me from across the field, a long blade of grass hanging out of the side of his mouth as he plots my demise. I changed his pink noodles for purple ones like Ranger suggested, but it hasn't seemed to improve the goat's disposition at all.

When we're a few feet from Doc, the donkey startles, then pauses his grazing to nudge my hand. Ranger strokes his fingers carefully along Doc's spine while Benny sniffs at the grass happily.

"I'm sorry," I blurt.

"Sorry," he says at the exact same time.

We both laugh.

"Wait. Why are *you* sorry?" he asks.

"For kissing you."

"That bad, huh?" His lips twist into an expression somewhere between a grimace and a smile, like even he's not sure if he's teasing or not.

"Too short to properly judge," I answer diplomatically. "But why are you apologizing?"

"I was pretty sure I was the one who did the kissing."

"You think so?" I lick my lips and forcibly focus my attention on petting Doc's forehead. If Ranger thinks *he's* the one who initiated the kiss, does that mean he *wanted* to kiss me? "I wasn't sure you were even gay."

"I'm not," he answers, and my heart sinks. "I think I'm bi."

I don't think I could stop my grin if I tried. I jerk my head up so fast I nearly give myself whiplash. But before I can say anything, he goes on.

"There was this guy, but..." He trails off, his expression

sober as he pinches the bridge of his nose. "I don't really want to talk about him."

I bob my head, burrowing my fingers again in Doc's fur to keep myself from reaching for Ranger.

"Okay, so we're two adults who just happened to kiss, initiator unknown," I conclude. "It doesn't have to ruin our friendship. We can pretend it didn't happen."

Now Ranger nods, his eyes seeming to be lost in a faraway world as he stares out over the field, his hand resting on the donkey's shoulder without moving. "What if I don't want to?"

"Don't want to...?"

"Pretend it didn't happen," he clarifies, snapping himself out of his thoughts and focusing his gaze on me, sharp and captivating. "I don't want to pretend it didn't happen."

"Oh." Fudge nuggets, my mouth is dry. I swallow and drag my sandpaper tongue over my lips again. Is he saying what I think he's saying? Is Ranger even in a place to want a relationship? Friendship is much safer for both of us. "So—"

This time there's no doubt about who kisses who. Ranger cuts off my words with his mouth on mine. Of course, all traces of cocoa are absent from his lips, but they still taste unbelievably sweet moving against mine. I wrap my arms around his neck and press myself closer, parting my lips to deepen the kiss. He seems to be on the same page and slips his tongue into my mouth, bunching the back of my shirt in his fists.

The hard bulge of his arousal meets mine, our bodies the right height to align perfectly. God, I've always loved a man I don't have to crane to kiss.

A hard ram to my backside breaks the moment, sending me toppling into Ranger, taking us both down with a hard *thud* and a muffled *oomph* against his mouth. The self-satisfied bleat leaves no mystery as to who was responsible for the attack.

"What the hell just happened?" he asks, looking up with a dazed expression as I heave myself off him.

"A drive-by goating," I answer with a deadpan expression, offering him my hand when I make it to my feet. We're lucky this didn't trigger an episode in him. Maybe because we were kissing? "Do you maybe want to come inside for a bit?"

It's a good thing Butler interrupted when he did. Ranger and I need to finish talking before we get to all the fun, naked parts. And holy frijoles, do I hope there will be fun, naked parts. Nipple-biting, cum-soaked, sweaty, naked parts. Damn, I need to focus.

I shake the deliciously filthy thoughts from my mind and wait for Ranger's answer.

"Yeah, that sounds good." He brushes the dirt off his jeans and eyes Butler suspiciously. The goat has returned to his grazing like nothing ever happened, the purple pool noodles on his horns bobbing up and down as he works his way through the field.

Ranger follows me inside, the dogs right behind us. Benny barks with excitement when he sees his siblings in the house, and a sweet smile forms on Ranger's lips.

"Do you think he misses them?" He nods towards the dogs as they wag and lick each other.

"Maybe on some level, but I think he's happy to have a new pack with you too," I assure him. "Do you want something to drink?"

"Just water," he says, and I point him to the couch, then escape into the kitchen to catch my breath, get my wits about me, and pour us both some water.

PP comes along as well and flops down onto the cool linoleum floor with a grunt.

"Good job keeping me from kissing him." I scoff, but she offers no apology, not even a contrite look. Some best friend she is. Although I can't say that kiss was the worst thing that ever happened. I just need to figure out where Ranger's head is and what it all means.

13
RANGER

As Julian marches to the kitchen, I sit on the couch, clenching and unclenching my hands, then swiping them over my thighs. I kissed him again... and he let me. That's a good sign, I tell myself as I anxiously await Julian's return from the kitchen. We were definitely on the same page out there, and I can't help but wonder what would've happened if we hadn't been interrupted by that goat.

Cockblocked by a goat. The absurdity of the whole thing hits me, and I chuckle. If I ever write a memoir, that would be the perfect title. I laugh even harder, and by the time Julian comes back, a worried look on his face, the tears are streaming down my face. Benny's eyes are full of concern as well, and I pat his head to signal I'm fine. I'm not fine, not in the bigger scheme of things, but right now, I choose to see the humor of a goat interrupting a hot kiss.

"You okay?" Julian asks. I really try to stop laughing, but it's hard. Unlike my cock, which has deflated, and that gives me another case of the giggles. When I finally have myself under control again, Julian's expression has changed from worry into something else. "I love seeing you laugh," he says.

"You can thank that stupid goat," I manage to say without breaking into a laughing fit again. Go me.

"Was that what you were laughing about?"

"I've decided that if I ever write a memoir, I'll call it 'Cockblocked by a Goat.'"

Julian chuckles, even if he rolls his eyes at the same time. "Butler is a menace, and he knows it."

"So why are you keeping him?"

Julian shrugs. "Because he's an animal who deserves to be taken care of. Things don't have to be perfect to deserve care and love."

I'm not oblivious to the deeper meaning in his words, and they warm my heart. "I'm far from perfect. In fact, I'm so damaged I don't think I'll even be whole again."

"Perfection is boring. Flaws are what make people interesting...or animals, for that matter."

He means it. I can't tell how I know that, but I do. Well, he has an ornery goat and a deaf donkey. That speaks volumes of his character. Not to mention that his husky has an interesting personality as well. She's been shooting daggers at Benny, who happily ignores it. Smart dog.

"So..." Julian says. "About that kiss..."

"The first one or the second one?"

A smile spreads over his face. "Either. Both. You said that you might be interested in more."

"More kisses? Yes, for sure. More of other things, also an option. But, Julian..." I have to be honest with him. He has to know what he's signing up for. "I'm not interested in anything more than casual fun."

Julian cocks his head, placing his index finger on his lips

as he studies me. "Casual sexy fun that includes the removal of clothes?"

"Preferably, yes."

"Sounds good. I'm in."

"Just like that?"

"What? You expected me to do a formal interview with you? Run a background check? It's not like I don't know anything about you."

He's got a point there, but still. This whole situation feels weird. Probably because I made it so with my way too-formal approach. For someone who insists on keeping things casual, I sure as fuck haven't managed to match my tone to that goal. "Right. Okay, then."

Julian's expression softens. "You don't have to talk about anything that's uncomfortable for you, but can you tell me if you've done this before?"

"Casual sex and hookups? Sure. It's all I've ever known. I've never had a serious relationship."

Julian holds my gaze. "With men?"

Ah, that. "No," I admit. "As you probably guessed, I hadn't fully come to terms with the fact that I'm bisexual."

Holy shit. I'm bisexual. It hits me all over again. Lucky once said that for those who aren't straight, the first years are a constant series of coming out, both to others and themselves, and I'm starting to see what he meant.

"You look like you just had an epiphany," Julian says.

I drag a hand through my hair. Damn, I need a haircut badly. "I may not have come fully to terms yet with me being bisexual," I rephrase my earlier statement.

Julian frowns. "Are you saying you're not bisexual? Or that maybe your brain isn't quite as ready as your body for the casual, naked fun?"

"No. I'm saying that I am, but that it still feels very new...

and really big. I knew, but it just now hit me again. My entire life, I've never considered myself to be anything else than straight, so to realize that I'm not is… It's still disorienting. My future has always implied a wife and kids, and this changes everything."

"Kids are still an option, you know," Julian says.

"I know. My brother, Lucky, the one who called you first? He's gay, and he has two partners. Trust me when I say that whatever I'm struggling with, it's not fueled by some latent homophobia."

"Okay."

Of course I've managed to change the direction of the discussion again and make it all heavy and depressing. Sometimes I feel like King Midas, except the things I touch don't become gold but turn dark and gloomy, much like my soul. And if that isn't the most pathetic crap ever, I don't know what is.

"I'm sorry."

"Sorry for what?"

I sigh. "For making it so heavy and complicated. I didn't mean to. This was supposed to be light and fun."

"I understand, but we're good. That being said, do you want to try it my way now?"

I nod eagerly. Whatever Julian has in mind has got to be better than my heavy-handed approach, right?

Julian jumps up from the couch and walks over to me. He gives me a second to become aware of what he's about to do, then climbs onto my lap and kisses me. No talk, no disclaimers, just his lips on mine.

I open up for him, letting him in, and I close my eyes as he sweeps his tongue into my mouth as if he owns it. He tastes like sunshine, like happiness, and I drink it in. He wraps his hands around my neck, and I put my hands on his back and pull him toward me until not a sheet of paper could fit between us. His tongue dances with mine, chasing me, then allowing me to conquer him before taking over again.

My stomach tickles, and nerves that have long been asleep fire up. Even jacking off had become too much effort lately, but now my cock is up and at 'em, ready for deployment.

I slip my hands under his shirt, moaning into his mouth when my rough fingers find his smooth skin. He's so pretty, so gorgeous, and I can't believe I'm allowed to touch him. He arches his back, leaning into my touch, and I let go of his mouth and kiss a trail of kisses toward his neck, his ear. He shivers, slowly grinding his groin against me.

"Can I touch you?" he whispers, and it takes me a second to realize why he's asking. I didn't ask him because to me, the consent was implied, considering he was on my lap. But he's checking to make sure because he doesn't want to trigger me. And that's so sweet and considerate, so classic Julian as how I've come to know him, that my stomach does a little somersault.

"Yes. Please."

He yips like a happy puppy as he shoves his hands under my shirt and caresses my back. His fingers are warm and gentle, tender as he explores my skin, going slow and easy. What would it feel like to have him play with my nipple barbell?

No man has ever touched me like this. Hell, no man has ever kissed me.

It should've been Alex. As much as I love kissing Julian —and god knows I do—I can't help but think that if I hadn't been such an idiot, I could've shared my first kiss with Alex.

The thought makes me freeze, and Julian carefully pulls

away. His eyes are full of concern as they meet mine. "Ranger?"

"Give me a moment," I say between clenched teeth, and he does, sitting perfectly still while I will the darkness away.

I sigh when I have myself under control again. "I'm sorry."

Julian climbs off my lap and takes a seat on the couch next to me. "It's okay."

"No, it's not. I wish I could tell you this won't happen again, but..."

"Ranger, I'm well aware. I've worked with veterans for a few years now, and I've seen what PTSD can do. I'm telling you it's okay. As long as you're open and honest with me, we can make this work."

Bitterness fills my mouth, a sharp contrast with Julian's sweet lips. "You could do so much better than me, even for casual sex."

Julian raises an eyebrow. "Your sales pitch needs some work, but you're a great kisser, and you're hot, so I'm willing to overlook that."

Huh? I snap my head up. Amusement sparkles in his gaze. Oh, he's teasing me, and my mouth curls up into a smile all on its own. "Thank you. I'll work on it, I promise."

"That's all I'll ever ask. Now, where were we?"

14

JULIAN

"Is that what it's supposed to look like?" I ask PP, frowning at my rather flat and possibly burned lasagna.

She lifts her head, sniffs the air, and then sneezes. Wow, with critique like that, I may have to stop letting her watch *Kitchen Nightmares* when I leave her home alone.

Sighing, I check the time on the stove clock. Ranger is going to be here any minute for our first planned "hangout." What said hangout entails is yet to be determined. Is he expecting me to answer the door wrapped in cellophane and immediately bend over for him? If he is, he might not be entirely on board with my "take things slow" plan.

I know *slow* and *casual* don't usually go together, but considering the bit of kissing last time nearly triggered him, not to mention his lack of experience, I'm not about to jump straight into bed with him.

"Maybe a home-cooked meal sends the wrong message." I pick up the spatula and poke at the blobby meal. "I don't want him to think I'm trying to push this into date territory."

PP grumbles and rolls onto her back as if belly rubs will solve everything. *Dogs*.

The doorbell rings, and my stomach flips. With one last helpless glance at my mutant lasagna, I wipe my hands on a rag and hurry to answer the door.

My breath catches at the sight of Ranger, freshly shaved, wearing a pair of dark wash jeans and a tight white T-shirt I can *totally* see the outline of his nipple piercing through. I don't give a bit of credence to virginity culture or any of that bull hockey, but the fact that I'm going to be the first man to ever touch him is a little intoxicating.

Fantasies fill my mind of dragging Ranger inside and straight down the hall to my bedroom, shoving him onto the bed and stripping him bare one item of clothing at a time, and then licking every inch of him until the only word he can remember is my name. My cock jerks and hardens against my thigh, and my throat goes dry.

"Can I come in?" He sounds uncertain and amused at the same time.

"Sorry, of course." I step aside and wave him in, Benny right at his side as they step into the house. "I wasn't sure if you planned to eat before coming over, so I made dinner. It's semiquestionable but likely edible," I tack on to prevent him from getting his hopes up too high.

"Semiquestionable but likely edible is my favorite," he teases.

"Lucky thing for both of us, then. Why don't you sit down and get comfortable, and I'll dish it up?" I gesture at the couch.

"Okay." His shoulders relax a bit. Benny is snuffling his hand and sticking close to him. Yeah, I'm not just imagining his tension. My plan to take things slow feels validated.

Tonight we can share dinner and watch a movie, maybe kiss some more, and everything else will come in time.

When I return to the living room with two plates of lasagna, Ranger sits on the couch, his shoes off, his ankle resting on his knee as he strokes Benny's head slowly.

"You have *Dogma*." He nods toward my shelf of movies. "I've been looking for that movie on Amazon for a while, but it's gone."

"Yeah, because of ducking Weinstein." I enjoy how his lips twitch in amusement at my use of the word *ducking*. "You want to watch it?"

"Sure."

I hand him his plate, then put mine down on the coffee table and set up the movie.

"Can I ask you a question?" Ranger asks when I pick up my plate and get comfortable on the couch next to him.

"Ask away."

"Why don't you swear? I don't mind. I'm just curious."

I chuckle. He's not the first one to give me strange looks about it, but he's the first person who's ever asked me. "It's more fun to come up with creative alternatives." I shrug.

"That's it? Because it's fun?" He furrows his eyebrows.

"Before I started working with animals, I was prelaw. My dad is a lawyer, so is my mom, my sister, my grandpa…" I'm sure he gets the picture. "I was halfway through my second year, and I realized I was completely miserable. I didn't want to wear a suit every day or memorize case law. They're happy, and that's good for them, but I wanted something different. This is *fun*." I wave my fork around. "Life's too short to do anything that isn't fun."

Ranger stares at me for approximately an eternity without saying a word. Then his mouth curves into a smile again. "I like you," he says, the simple words warming me all over.

"I like you too." I reach over slowly and pat his knee.

I hit Play on the movie, and we both dig into our food. Based on the sounds he makes, it must not be the worst lasagna he's ever had. It's a little crunchy around the edges but definitely passable.

Our shoulders bump while we eat and laugh together at the movie. We have a brief debate about whether or not angels have buttholes, since they don't have genitals, and whether or not Ben Affleck's character *grows* a dick once his wings are destroyed and he's no longer an angel.

When we're finished eating, Ranger follows me into the kitchen, where I fill up the sink. He offers to dry the dishes, which is awfully domestic for a casual hookup, but I'm not about to point that out to him.

When everything is washed, dried, and put away, a fresh awareness starts to crackle between us. Ranger licks his lips, and my eyes linger on the dampness of his mouth. I reach out and put my hand on the center of his chest, feeling his erratic heartbeat against my palm and watching his Adam's apple bob as he swallows hard, his eyes fixed on me intensely. Staring as a form of foreplay? That's a new one, but based on how quickly my dick is getting hard, it's effective.

He steps closer, backing me against the counter and resting his forehead against mine. I curl my fingers around the fabric of his shirt, slowly putting the other on his arm, and nuzzle his nose. My heart flails as wildly as his, my skin prickling at the closeness, my body aching for his kiss as his breath fans over my lips.

Nothing about this feels casual, but I do everything in my power to keep my mind from going there. He wants a bit of fun, a chance to explore his sexuality in a safe way, and I can give him that. I *want* to give him that.

I surge forward, closing the space between our mouths. Ranger's soft moan vibrates against my lips, his tongue slipping into my mouth and tangling with mine. He sneaks his hands under my shirt, teasing my skin with his calloused fingers. My dick aches for more of his touch. His erection is pressed against mine, my jeans dulling the feeling but not dousing it completely.

It doesn't take long for the kiss to go from tentative exploration to hot and heavy probing, our tongues sliding against each other, teeth nipping, hands everywhere, breaths harsh.

"Do you want to…" Ranger murmurs against my mouth, and I groan. I don't know his intended end to that sentence, but whatever it is, I have no doubt that I *really* want to. Unfortunately, some distant part of my brain reminds me of my plan to take this slowly.

"There's no rush. This is nice." I kiss along his jaw. "But I wouldn't be opposed to relocating for a little more comfort."

His fingers dance along my waist, and he nods. When he steps back, both Benny and PP stand a few feet away, staring at us.

"If I'd realized we were putting on a show, I might've hammed it up a bit more," I joke.

"Benny, lie down," Ranger says, giving him the signal to stand down for now. I drag Ranger back to the couch, leaving the dogs in the kitchen.

The movie is paused, the screen frozen with Matt Damon's face, but we ignore it completely, tumbling onto the couch together, Ranger on top of me as our mouths crash into each other again.

Slow doesn't have to mean boring, and I make it my

mission to show him that by sucking a mark onto the base of his throat while I flick his nipple stud with my thumb. He moans, grinding his hips against me, the hard ridge of his cock aligned perfectly with mine.

We kiss and touch but keep things pretty PG-13, all our clothes remaining more or less in place. I have no idea how long we make out on the couch like horny teenagers, but when we finally break apart, my lips are sore, and my balls are aching, neither of which I'm complaining about.

As if in silent agreement, we sit up straight and continue to watch the movie. He puts his arm along the back of the couch, and I lean in close enough that to the untrained eye, we might appear to be cuddling. But casual hookups don't cuddle, which I remind myself of throughout the rest of the movie and long after Ranger has gone home for the night, leaving me with my right hand and his name on my lips, both of which are used to exhaustion before I fall asleep.

15

RANGER

I'm getting better at this whole I-need-help thing, I think as I press on the green button on my phone and call my friend David. We haven't talked in a while, but I know he won't hold that against me. I texted him earlier today that I wanted to talk, and he gave me a good time to reach him.

"Ranger," he says, his voice warm. "I'm so glad you called."

"You don't even know what I need from you," I quip.

David chuckles. "Unless you'd ask for my firstborn, I'm pretty sure you couldn't ask for a thing I wouldn't give you."

Did I mention David is a genuinely good guy? As a criminal defense attorney, he helped Heart get a retrial and get his sentencing reversed last year. For free, even though both Lucky and I offered to pay him.

"Dude, you don't even have a child."

"Like that's ever mattered in any of the fairy tales. I'm just saying I won't sign over the rights to my firstborn."

Ranger laughed. "Good to know, but that's not what I'm

after. I just need your advice on something. Something personal. But let's catch up first. How have you been?"

"Mack Stone," David says, his tone strict, and yet I smile because I know he's messing with me. "If you honestly think we're gonna talk about the weather and all that crap when you drop a bomb like that, you're sorely mistaken. You need personal advice? You shall have it. Hit me with it."

He's joking, but not entirely. I've rarely come to him for personal advice, so he's well aware of how special this occasion is. But how do I segue into what I want to ask him? Is there a natural way to go from "How have you been?" to "By the way, I'm bi, and I have questions?"

I doubt there is, but I have to ease into this. "How's your boyfriend?" I ask, unable to think of something better.

"My boyfriend? Which one? I think you're about three boyfriends behind, but my latest one, Adam, is nice. He's cute, tolerably conceited, and his ass is the stuff of wet dreams. Besides, he gives great head, but I'm sure you don't need to hear the details."

I close my eyes for a moment. "What if I do?" The line grows deadly silent, and I check my phone to make sure we haven't been disconnected. "David?"

"Did you just ask me for details on my boyfriend's oral skills?"

"More, like, tips?" I say sheepishly.

"Ranger, I know for a fact you've had blow jobs. I was there quite a few times. So why on earth would you need me to give you tips on... Oh. *Oh.*"

I take a deep breath. "I'm bi."

"You're bi."

"Yes. Pretty sure."

"We've known each other for how long now? Twenty-two years?"

We met in high school and became instant best friends, so that sounds about right. "Yeah."

"And you've waited this long to tell me you're bi when I could've done all my experimenting with you rather than with Nick Williamson? The fuck, man?"

It's a classic David reaction, and I can't help but laugh. "Sorry. I was a little slow."

"Yeah, I'll say. I've lusted after you for years, so this is highly disappointing."

"You've lusted after me?"

"God, Ranger, have you seen yourself? Every person on the planet would kill to sleep with you, straight, bi, gay, or anything else. But rest assured, it was a safe lusting. Nothing I would've ever acted on in person. Though if you're declaring your undying love for me, I'll jump into the car right now and show up on your doorstep within two hours. Naked and horny as fuck. What do you say?"

And this is why we're best friends. He has the unique skill of breaking the tension and making everything seem lighter and easier. "Tempting, but no," I say with a smile.

"Bummer. But why the shift in sexual orientation?"

The laugh on my lips fades. "I met someone...and lost him."

"Oh, Mack..." David's tone changes instantly, and his words wrap around me like a hug. "I'm so sorry."

"Yeah. He was... He was special." I clear my throat. "Anyway, so... Yeah, bisexual."

"Welcome to the rainbow, man. I love having you...and your brother must've been thrilled."

"I think he's more relieved that I'm doing better."

"Are you? Doing better, I mean?"

"Yes. Yes, I am. Lucky hooked me up with a charity that provides vets with a service dog, and that's how I got Benny.

I'll send you a pic after, but he's a golden retriever, and he's become my best buddy. I'm working with his trainer, Julian, and it's been a lifechanger for me."

"And I'm gonna take a wild guess and say Julian is gay? And single?"

I'm not even gonna ask how he knows. We're talking about a man who reads people for a living and is basically the human equivalent of a lie detector. "Yeah. I'm not ready for a relationship, but I'm hoping to have some fun with him. The kind of fun where we take our clothes off. And when we do, I don't wanna look like an idiot who doesn't know what he's doing…"

"And you don't want to talk sex with your brother," David says, sounding like he completely understands. "Even though he's in a relationship with a former porn star who knows more about sex than anyone we know."

Okay, so maybe he doesn't.

For a fleeting moment I consider reaching out to Heart, but then reality sets in. I can't do that. I don't know him well enough to know how he feels about his porn star career, so asking him may stir up all kinds of bad memories. I won't do that to him. Besides, I'm not sure how Lucky would feel about being reminded of his boyfriend's past. He's never seemed to have an issue with it, but I'm not causing trouble for him if I can prevent it.

"Yeah."

"Okay, I get it. You've come to the right place because there's little I don't know about gay sex. Hit me with it."

A few years from now, I may look back on this conversation and see the humor in it, but right now, I'm ten kinds of mortified. But not embarrassed enough to forget about the whole thing. "I've watched plenty of gay porn, so I'm well aware of the mechanics of it."

"Porn isn't realistic. I hope you know that. They skip a lot of important steps, like consent and prep."

I nod, even though David can't see that. "Right. I'd gathered as much. But I have a different question. How do you determine...roles? How do you bring that up?"

"Good question," David says and his serious tone makes clear he's not gonna give me grief over this, bless him. "The biggest mistake you can make is assuming. Just because someone has a certain body type doesn't mean they prefer the role associated with that. Like me, I mostly prefer to top, even though I'm often mistaken for a bottom."

I cringe. Did I really need to know that? On the other hand, I have to applaud him for being transparent and honest with me.

"So the best thing is to simply ask. Very few men will be offended if you bring it up as an open question. Like, do you prefer to top or to bottom, or are you vers?"

"Vers?"

"Versatile, meaning you like both. I'm somewhat vers because I'm not opposed to bottoming for the right guy, but it's not my first preference. Other men are completely top or bottom...or they don't like anal sex at all. There are a lot of fun things to do if that's the case. Anal is not the end-all, just to be clear."

I frown. Was I wrong to assume Julian wants anal sex? He seemed to have hinted at it, but David is right. I'd better double-check. "Okay. Let's say we do want that. What do I need to know? What's the stuff no one tells you?"

David is quiet for a moment. "That it can be beautiful but also disappointing. That sometimes your body doesn't cooperate. That it can be messy and embarrassing in terms of sounds and fluids and stuff, but also wonderfully intimate and special. That it feels really good when it's done right but awful when it goes wrong. That you need a lot of communication to make it good, a lot of openness...or a lot of experience."

"I don't want to disappoint him...let him down," I say softly. "I already have so little to offer him, so this has to work."

"You're putting an awful lot of pressure on yourself, bro. You're also wrong. You're an amazing man, and anyone would be lucky to have you, regardless of their gender."

The sigh I let out seems to come from my soul. "I'm broken, man. Damaged. I'm not the Ranger you knew."

"You forget that I knew you before you were Ranger..." David's voice is infinitely kind and warm. "You were Mack when we met, just another high schooler. You were kind and strong and smart, and that hasn't changed. You're still Mack, even if you can't be Ranger anymore. You know what I'm saying?"

My throat is tight. "Yeah."

"You'll find your way, Mack. I know you will. And I'm here, no matter what you need. Legal advice, a listening ear, all the tips on gay sex... I'm even willing to drive to your house and give you some personal instruction on how to give a good blow job."

Ah, there's the foolish David again. "I love you, man." I swallow, my emotions still dangerously close to the surface.

"I love you too, bro. Glad I can finally tell you that after twentysome years, no kidding."

He'll always make me laugh but in the best way. "At least I know your love will pass the test of time...and distance. Anyway, talk to me about what's happening in your life."

"No more sex questions? Damn."

"I'm sure I'll think of some later."

16

JULIAN

"Now look what you've done." I gesture at the broken fence Butler doesn't seem the least bit sorry about. He bleats and lowers his head, clearly trying to decide whether he wants to ram me or not for daring to scold him. "It's fine." I hold my hands up defensively. "I can fix it. No harm, no foul."

I hate fixing fences. I can do it in a pinch, but I always get blisters and lose a whole day working on it, plus it makes me crabby. I sigh. Is it worth it to call in someone else to fix it, or should I suck it up and do it myself?

First things first. I need to move Doc and Butler into the horse pasture until I can get this fence repaired. Doc isn't particularly fond of the horses, but I also don't want to leave him bored in the barn all day, so I don't have many other options.

"Come on, guys." I attempt to herd them toward the gate that connects the two pastures. Butler leaps onto the wooden jungle gym instead, and Doc continues munching on grass, completely oblivious to the fact that I want him to go anywhere else. I'm a good animal trainer, I swear.

The silly goat has been rather attached to Doc lately, so if I can get the donkey to move, I have a feeling Butler will follow.

"I'm going to get your halter. Don't go anywhere while I'm gone," I tell Doc sternly, not bothering to sign it. He's not looking at me anyway.

Hurrying into the barn, I try to remember where I hung his halter and lead. My phone buzzes in my pocket, and a smile jumps instantly to my face. I have no reason to think it'll be Ranger other than that we've continued texting regularly since he came over a few nights ago. Except this isn't a text; it's a call. It might be a potential client or maybe Rick calling to let me know about a new batch of puppies, since all of Benny's littermates have gone to needy vets now. I pull it out and answer without looking.

"Hello?"

"Hey."

Ranger's voice on the other end sends a little thrill through me. It's strange he calls instead of texting, though. "Is everything okay?"

"Yeah. Just finished up my morning yoga. I was lying here petting Benny and thinking about you."

He was thinking about me? That doesn't sound like something a casual hookup would say. Then again, all this is new to him, so maybe I need to take anything he says with a grain of salt.

"Lucky you. I'm not doing anything quite that relaxing."

"Oh? What are you up to?"

"Trying to remember where I put Doc's halter so I can move his stubborn caboose over to the horse pasture until I can fix his fence." I spot the pink-and-blue-striped lead hanging off one of the stalls and cheer internally.

"What happened to the fence?"

"Butler," I grumble. "You know, maybe he's lonely, and that's why he's acting out. I could get him a girlfriend...or a boyfriend. I suppose I should get both so he can choose for himself. I wouldn't want to make any assumptions on his behalf."

Ranger chuckles, the sound warm and inviting. "You want to get *more* goats?"

"Not particularly. But I don't want Butler to be unhappy. He deserves to live his best life."

He's quiet for a minute, and I wonder what he's thinking. "I could fix the fence," he offers, surprising me.

"What? You don't have to do that."

"I want to. It was actually kind of fun building the fence here, even if it took me a lot longer than I planned. I bet I could fix yours easily."

I weigh his offer while I head back out into the field, relieved to see both the boys are where I left them. "Give me a minute," I say, sticking my phone into my pocket without waiting for his response.

Doc finally lifts his head, and as soon as he sees the halter, his ears go back. He lets out a noisy bray and immediately starts walking in the opposite direction, which is fortunate because it's exactly the direction I want him moving in. I keep walking toward him, staying out of kicking and biting range while holding out the halter as a way of motivating him to keep going. As predicted, once Butler sees what's happening, he jumps down off his jungle gym and trots over to join the fun.

"That's right. Go play with the horses," I coo, unlatching the gate and shooing them through.

With that done, I drape the halter and lead around my neck and bring my phone back to my ear.

"Sorry about that. If you're sure you want to come over and fix the fence, it would certainly help me out a ton."

"Great." Ranger sounds genuinely excited at the prospect. "I'll be there in a bit."

"Okay, thanks again."

While I wait for Ranger to arrive, I finish up with my morning chores, cleaning out the chicken coop and feeding the girls. When I step inside, I notice they're not as active as usual, all perched in the back of the coop instead of running around like they normally do this time of day.

I sniff the air. The Segura wildfire has been burning for two days now. Is it already affecting the air quality here? Chickens, well, birds in general, have much more sensitive respiratory tracts than humans, so even a little bit of smoke or ash in the air can cause them distress.

I don't smell anything, but I'll have to keep a close eye on them. The news said it was a small fire at the moment, and it's far enough away that I'm not too worried, but one thing I've learned since moving out here is that wildfires can go from minor to holy shnikes in a very short amount of time.

~

I ANTICIPATED that having Ranger fix the fence would mean I'd have time to work with Bella, my tan mare, who has a commercial spot coming up next week. What I didn't anticipate was that the man would be shirtless...*again*.

On my signal, Bella rears up, whinnying and tossing her head majestically. It's going to look fantastic on film, but I'm barely paying attention to her because Ranger. Is. Shirtless. *Again*.

"Do you think he's doing this on purpose?" I give her a

carrot and pat her nose. "If he came over here to seduce me, all he had to do was say so."

She snorts and nuzzles my palm, looking for more treats. "Take a break," I tell her, giving the side of her neck a little push. She bumps me with her nose one more time, then trots off. I climb over the fence, definitely not trying to look like a cool cowboy or anything in case he's watching, and saunter through the pasture to where Ranger is working with Benny resting in the shade a few feet away.

He doesn't seem quite as skinny as he did when we first met. His skin has a little bit more color to it too, which I'm willing to bet is the result of him spending time outside with Benny.

The beads of sweat on his back beckon me to lick them off, and that's not where my fantasies end. By the time I reach him, I'm fully hard, a prominent bulge in my jeans.

"How's it going?"

He glances over his shoulder and grins at me.

"Almost finished."

I crane to peer past him. The fence does indeed look just about back in tip-top shape.

"That was fast. This would've taken me most of the day."

He furrows his brow. "It's just cutting wood and nailing it together."

"Yes, but you have to factor in time for splinters, losing the hammer, a trip to urgent care when I smash my thumb. It's a whole production," I explain, and he laughs.

"Well, I'm happy to help out if you need it." He finishes hammering the last nail into place and then stands up. I drool shamelessly over the flex and stretch of the muscles in his back as he uses his arm to wipe sweat from his face.

"Will you be shirtless the whole time?" I let my voice dip

low, along with my eyes, which linger on the perky curve of his butt.

"If you want."

"Mmm, in that case, something in the barn just broke." I manage to tear my eyes off his bouncy behind and back up to his face. He arches an eyebrow.

"Is that so? What exactly is this new broken item?"

"I'll have to show you. It's very technical and...*hard*." I lick my lips. "Hard to fix, I mean."

"By all means, then, we'd better go check it out."

Ranger gives Benny the signal to stay, and then the two of us dart off to the barn like the farmhand and the heiress in a tawdry historical romance.

Once we're inside, I lead him to the feed room, where bales of hay and alfalfa are stacked high against the walls. I've always wanted to fool around with someone in here, and I'm about to *carpe* the cluck out of this *diem*.

"The broken thing is over there." I point vaguely, biting back the wicked smile threatening to give me away. Not that I think for one second that Ranger isn't onto me, but pretending is half the fun.

"Over here?" He wanders in the direction I indicated.

"Mmhmm." I close the door behind us and follow him deeper into the room.

"Where exactly?" he asks, turning back toward me when he reaches the smaller stack of hay bales.

"Right here." I grab the back of his neck and crash my mouth into his.

17

RANGER

Julian's kiss is eager and hungry without showing any hesitation. His hand unashamedly pulls my head toward his, and I love it. Almost as much as I appreciated the way he was ogling me, not even masking he wasn't checking me out. It feels good.

His tongue slips between my lips, invading my mouth, sweet and seductive. He tastes fresh, minty, as if he's had Tic Tacs or something. But he's also uniquely Julian, with that flavor that's all him: sunshine and happiness.

I hesitate for a moment, then wrap my arms around him and cup his ass. That luscious ass I've dreamed of. He rewards me by plastering his body against mine, and all my senses are full of him. How he feels just right in my arms, his sweet taste, his intoxicating smell, the hot sounds he makes as we kiss and kiss and kiss.

He's taking his time, thoroughly exploring my mouth, and I'm just as eager to do the same to him. I love how he's careful in his moves, always signaling his intent by halting just a fraction, giving me time to mentally get ready...or to say no. Consent really is sexy, I'm telling you.

When he gently pushes against my chest, I get the hint, and we stumble backward and drop onto a pile of hay, Julian on top of me. Thank fuck I don't have hay fever. The hay is rough against my bare skin, but it smells amazing, and who would've known a tumble in the hay would actually be hot? Then again, I suspect anything would be hot when it's Julian kissing me.

His body covers mine everywhere, and I *like* it. I've never had a man on top of me, and it's different. Harder, not the soft curves of a woman. And yet it doesn't feel unfamiliar or strange at all. We fit like two pieces of a puzzle, our bodies all but melding together.

I knead his ass as we continue the kiss, stealing breaths from each other's mouths as we chase and capture, pursue and surrender. The small sounds he makes in the back of his throat are encouraging, as is the unmistakable pressure of his hard dick against my body. Another new sensation for me, but it feels wonderfully right.

His jeans are tight, which makes his ass pop like you wouldn't believe, but it does pose a challenge when I try to wriggle one hand under his waistband. The damn pants are so tight I only get three fingers in, and even if they're long, it's not nearly enough to touch as much of him as I want to.

Julian doesn't break off the kiss but rolls to one side and, with his left hand, opens the button on his jeans and unzips it. I appreciate a man who can multitask.

"Mmm, better." I sigh into his mouth and slip a hand under his underwear. His skin feels warm and smooth under my rough fingers, and I caress him almost reverently. He's so...pretty. Beautiful. Gorgeous.

Not in any way like Alex, who was a tough soldier, his body as trained as mine, and nothing but solid muscles. Not that I ever got the chance to kiss him or even hold him, but he wouldn't have felt the same. Julian is so much smaller and leaner, and even though I know he's not fragile, he feels as if I can break him in two.

"You good?" Julian asks, and I blink. When did we stop kissing?

"Yeah. I was just...thinking of how pretty you are."

His face breaks open in a wide smile. "Look at you, flirting like a pro."

"Is it flirting if it's the truth?"

He winks at me. "It is if you say it in that low, sexy voice of yours."

"You like my voice?"

"Frack, yes. Have you heard yourself? Well, of course you have, but your own voice always sounds weird because it's in your head. But trust me on this. You have an incredibly sexy voice, perfect for whispering dirty things in my ear."

No one has ever made me feel the way he does. Hot. Wanted. Desirable, even with all my hang-ups and weaknesses—weaknesses he's probably more aware of than anyone else. Like I'm worthy of his affection. "Dirty things? Like what?"

"Oh, I don't know... You could tell me what you're feeling or thinking right now that's got you so hard..."

He grinds his hips down on my erection, and a low moan flies from my lips. God, that feels incredible.

"Or you could fantasize about what you'd like to do to me and describe it to me in detail. Splendid, sexy detail..."

I swallow. Pictures flood my brain of Julian riding me, his head thrown back and his face showing nothing but pleasure as my cock fills him to the max. His sweet lips wrapped around my cock, his eyes fixed on mine as he takes me deep into his mouth. Me jacking myself off and coming all over him. Marking his skin with my cum...

I swear I have no idea when I became that guy, the kind of man who gets all possessive and primitive.

"Ranger, we'll do whatever you're comfortable with." His voice has lost its teasing tone. I've stayed silent too long. He must think he's scaring me or going too fast.

I bring my lips close to his ear, then blow out a soft breath. He shivers. "I want to do everything to you..."

"God, yes, please. Whatever you want, I volunteer as tribute."

Leave it to Julian to make me smile, even when I'm seconds away from ripping his clothes off and burying myself inside him. But I don't want to rush this. I want to savor this experience and not just because it's my first time with another man. It feels too special to hurry. Something tells me that every step of this journey will be worth it, and it would be a shame to skip ahead.

I lift my hips and, at the same time, push his ass downward, creating delicious pressure on my dick. My moan mingles with Julian's strangled groan. "Do that again," he says breathily.

While I undulate my hips, I catch his bottom lip between my teeth and gently pull it out, then let it go with a plop. His cheeks flush, and his eyes darken as they bore into mine. "Ranger..." he whispers.

This time, Julian grinds his body down on mine with a slow move, his eyes never leaving mine. His cheeks are burning, his lips wet and red, and he's never looked prettier. I catch his lips in another kiss, and then we both multitask, our tongues and lips twirling in the same rhythm as our bodies.

Not another word is spoken as we chase our pleasure, sliding and grinding against each other in an erotic dance unlike any I've ever participated in. Our joint gasps and moans fill the barn, and sweat beads on my skin. The pressure is exquisite, and the tension in my body is building up with every twist of my hips, every swirl of his.

My hand is still on his bare ass, and my fingers find his hole, which I imagine will be as pretty as the rest of him. I wait a beat, but when he only moans, I press two fingers against his entrance. I greedily swallow the needy sound Julian makes.

He moans, bucking his hips uncontrolled, seeking more pressure. Our breaths speed up, our kisses now sloppy and breathy, and Julian's eyes are closed.

My balls feel full and heavy, tingling with need, and it won't take much more to send me over the edge. My movements are driven by instinct, by the need to come, and they're far from coordinated anymore. I just need...more. A bit more friction. Our bodies become frantic, sliding and pressing against each other. I'm so fucking close, every cell in me hurtling toward release.

"I'm right on the edge," Julian pants.

"Me too," I manage.

He opens his eyes, meeting my gaze with naked desire and, surprisingly, tenderness. "Let's fly, baby."

I let go, groaning loudly as I circle my hips upward with force one last time, and then my orgasm breaks free. It rolls over me like a tsunami, making my body shake from my toes to the crown of my head. My trapped cock releases, and I grunt as my balls squeeze out every last drop. I only faintly register Julian tensing up and then shuddering as well, his body jerking against mine.

For a moment, I feel like I'm falling, and panic claws at me, but then his lips are on mine, and he pulls me back in with a slow, deep kiss. When we finally break apart, my underwear is all sticky, and I grimace.

Julian chuckles. "Coming in your pants always sounds amazing...until about a minute later."

"Right? But was it? Amazing, I mean?"

His smile is soft as he kisses me on my lips, then scrambles up. "That was hot as fudge."

"It was," I agree.

We look at each other as we're standing, and then we burst out in laughter. "You somewhat resemble a scarecrow," Julian says. "A sexy one, admittedly, but you have hay everywhere."

He's a little better, but it still takes us at least two minutes to get the worst of the hay off him. Even then, I still look like I just took a tumble in the hay, which I did, so whatever.

"Wanna freshen up inside?" Julian asks.

I shoot him a doubtful look. "Not sure this can be salvaged with a quick wash."

His breath catches, and his eyes flash. "We could take a shower together?"

18

JULIAN

My lips are tingling from our rough kisses, and every inch of my skin feels oversensitive and raw like I might fly apart into a million pieces at any second. Despite all that, my cock has only partially deflated, more than ready for a second round if Ranger is up for it.

I lace my fingers through his, my heart fluttering at the smile that tilts his lips. Casual fun includes fluttering hearts, right? I totally have this under control. I can't resist pressing another quick kiss to his mouth, memorizing the shape of his smile before tugging him along out of the barn and up to the house.

Benny joins us, still at ease since Ranger gave him the signal to stand down earlier, but always on alert, making sure his human doesn't need him. The dog no doubt sees the same thing I do: loose movements, a relaxed, happy expression that doesn't seem to grace Ranger's face often enough. He's even sexier like this, more himself. I'm not under any delusion that playing with my dick cured his

PTSD, but it's nice to think that the fun we're having can settle his demons for a few minutes at a time at least.

When we get into the house, Ranger directs Benny to the living room, then lets me tow him down the hall to the bathroom, the two of us trading kisses and bumping into the walls along the way. He chuckles against my mouth, the sound vibrating through me and lighting me up from head to toe.

We manage to make it to the bathroom, and I kick the door closed behind us before pushing him up against the sink, only breaking our kiss long enough to pull my shirt off and toss it onto the floor.

Every time we crash back together, the kiss somehow feels more frantic, more desperate, hungrier. My cock is fully hard again, pressing against Ranger's answering steel. At least we know we have compatible sex drives, which is the most important thing to find in a casual hookup.

Casual, casual, casual. All good.

Ranger groans when I break the kiss so I can start the shower and have a few seconds to catch my breath.

"You have a paw print tattoo on your shoulder." He gently drags his index finger along the back of my shoulder, and goose bumps pop up all over my skin as he traces the shape of my first and only tattoo.

"It's an imprint of my first dog's paw. When I was a kid, I wanted a dog so bad, but my mom was *not* about that life. Fast-forward to my second year as a prelaw student. One night I was walking back to my dorm from the library. It was freezing and had just started to snow. I stopped at a crosswalk, and while I was waiting for the signal to change, I noticed that on the other side of the road, a dog was tied to a tree. I scanned around, expecting to see an owner, and when I didn't, I headed straight over to her. It was obvious she'd been abandoned there on purpose. She was whining, covered in her own pee, and shivering in the cold. When I cut her loose, she tried to bite me, but as soon as she was free, she started licking my hand and tried to jump on me."

My throat tightens at the memory. With jerky movements, I strip out of my pants and underwear, letting them fall onto the pile of clothes on the tile floor. Nothing kills an erection like talking about your dead dog. *Smooth, Julian.*

Ranger takes off his pants as well. I reach into the shower to check the temperature of the water before pulling back the curtain all the way and waving him in. He steps under the spray and groans, tilting his head back to catch the water on his face and then moves aside so I can get in too.

"So, what happened?" he asks once I'm in the shower with him.

"I brought her back to my dorm and paid my roommate twenty bucks not to rat me out to the RA." I smile as I think back to the week I spent hiding Layla in my dorm, sneaking food back, and begging her not to bark. "One night, I couldn't get her to keep quiet, and when the RA came by to find out what was going on, I pretended I had a cough that just sounded like a dog barking."

Ranger laughs, and I join him, reaching for the bottle of body wash perched on the ledge and pouring some into my hands.

"Why didn't you just say you were watching a movie with a dog barking?" he asks.

"Well, snickerdoodles, where were you back then?" Without thinking twice, I lather up my hands and run them over his chest and shoulders, catching his nipple piercing against my palm and sending a shudder through him.

"Hmmm, probably Afghanistan?" he muses, all humor

gone from his voice. I bite the inside of my cheek, praying I didn't just ruin the moment. But then he leans into my touch and meets my eyes again. "Then what happened?"

"Shockingly, the RA didn't buy my lie. The next day I got a notice that I had to get rid of her or vacate the dorms. It wasn't even a question. I packed up my stuff and dropped my classes. I was already unhappy anyway, and having to choose between housing and Layla just sealed the deal. I guess she changed my life. She was like my angel, my little terrorist angel." I pause, caught between my memories and this moment with my soapy hands all over Ranger's body. "Boy, did that dog love to destroy my stuff, but I got her under control eventually, and learning how to handle her is how I got interested in animal training and behavior. The rest is history."

He hums in acknowledgment, bending his head for a softer kiss this time, our lips moving slowly against each other, our wet bodies slipping and sliding together. I moan against his mouth, my cock surging back to life against his, bumping and grinding together, the kiss heating up.

Ranger drags his fingers through my wet hair, backing me up against the wall, the tile cool compared to the heat of the water and his body. The contrasting temperatures light all my nerve endings on fire. I sink my fingers into his back, nipping at his bottom lip and thrusting against him.

Our grunts and groans echo off the shower walls, the head of my cock catching against his with each thrust, and the sticky remnants of our first orgasms mix with fresh precum and the water cascading over us.

"Fuck," he gasps, his nose bumping against mine. Our kisses turn sloppy as we hump against each other like wild animals in heat.

"Ranger," I pant his name against his mouth, digging my

fingers harder into his muscles as my balls tighten, and my cock pulses against his. Without warning, my orgasm crashes over me, my cum coating his cock and my own before being washed away by the water.

He lets out a strangled sound, thrusting his hips erratically as his release joins mine.

As our orgasms fade, our kisses and groping hands slow, our chests heaving against each other. My throat is raw from moaning, and my balls are sore from two orgasms so close together, but I still want to lick this man from head to toe.

Ranger pulls away and plucks the bottle of body wash off the ledge, then fills his hands just like I did.

"I told you my story. Have you any of your own to share?" I ask softly, watching him form a lather in his hands to wash the rest of the cum, dust, and sweat off my body.

"A story?" He sounds amused and slightly exhausted at the same time.

"No pressure." My eyes fall closed as he gently slides his hands all over my skin.

"Okay, I've got one," he says after a few seconds. "When I was around ten, my brother Lucky and I…"

I sag into his touch, listening to him tell me about his childhood, soaking up the happiness in his tone, and reminding myself over and over again that he wants this to be casual.

19

RANGER

I'm warm in my uniform, way too warm, sweating like crazy. The sun is burning down on me, and all I can think of is a cold can of Coke.

"I'd fucking kill for a beer," Alex says, wiping his brow.

"No can do, Brooklyn. Now shut up and focus," I say, and he reacts by winking at me.

His cheeky grin makes my heart warm and my cock hard, and I want to kiss it off his face. He's so goddamn beautiful, and he knows it too, but it's all part of his charm.

He's still smiling when the bullet hits him, and then I'm covered in blood as I try to make it stop, but I can't. His eyes stare at me, devoid of life, and I scream and scream and scream.

I wake up hyperventilating, my body drenched in sweat, shaking with tremors as Benny licks my face and has two paws on my chest. He whines, and I sink my hands into his fur, holding on to him for god knows how long until my breathing is finally under control and my body has stopped shivering.

I can barely think, my head pounding like a platoon of

marching soldiers as it often does after a nightmare. I don't know if it's because of hyperventilating and too much oxygen in my system or from something else, but every time I wake up in the middle of one, I feel like I got run over by a goddamn tank.

"That was a bad one," I tell Benny, whose eyes are full of kindness and understanding. Don't ever tell me dogs don't know what's going on. He damn well knows I'm suffering, and all he wants is to make me feel better.

The clock tells me it's three AM, and my chances of getting more sleep are zero, so I might as well get up. I force myself out of my bed, which is soaked from my sweat. "Gonna take a shower." Benny follows me into the bathroom, apparently determined not to leave me out of his sight. I don't think he trusts that I'm okay, and I gotta admit that he's probably right.

The lukewarm shower helps cool me off and refresh, and by the time I towel myself off, I'm feeling slightly more human, though still unsteady. I sigh when I walk into the bedroom and see the crumpled, dirty linens. No way do I have the energy to change those now, so instead, I grab a blanket and head over to the couch in the living room, making a quick detour through the kitchen to get a bottle of water. I'm not gonna sleep anyway, so the plan is to watch some TV.

The Home Shopping Network and I have become close friends over the last year. In my defense, I've only bought four things, and so far, they turned out pretty good. One was actually much better than I had expected, some weird Teflon-coated defrosting rack that rapidly defrosts meat. I thought it was BS but put a frozen steak on there, and it's really defrosted three times as fast. And no, I don't want to talk about the fact that I've become the kind of person who is excited over defrosting steak.

I lie on the couch, Benny snuggled close to me, and mindlessly flip through the channels. I watch half a rerun of House—why the fuck would they broadcast that in the middle of the night?—then catch the last forty-five or so minutes from one of the Fast & Furious movies, and before I know it, dawn is breaking, and I've survived another night. Yay me.

I've lost count of the number of nights I've spent like this, but it's been a lot. Though I have to admit this was the first nightmare in a while. I've been sleeping better lately. As soon as I wonder why, I immediately have the answer: Julian and Benny. Or Benny and Julian. I never knew that having a dog in bed with me would make a difference, but it does. He's like a stuffed animal, only real.

And Julian is... As soon as I think of him, my lips curve up in a smile. He's sweet and funny, and hanging out with him has been amazing. We've had one more meetup since our tumble in the hay—a highly satisfying mutual hand job session. I think I'm ready for more, but I'm not sure how to go about it. Do I flat out ask him? Like, hey, J, can I blow you?

I wince. It sounds so blunt. Surely there has to be a sexier way to approach this. I check the clock. Six fifteen. He'll be awake, Mr. Corporate Hotshot Lawyer.

Ranger: How do I ask someone if they want a blow job?

David: I can be there in an hour.

I snort.

Ranger: Not you, asshole.

David: I'm willing to sacrifice myself in the name of your research.

Ranger: How honorable of you.

David: I know. And I do have a pretty nice dick if I do say so myself.

Ranger: I'll take your word for it.

David: You sure? Happy to send you a pic...

He cracks me up. It's a rare combination, someone as smart as he is with his silly sense of humor. It's funny because in a way, he reminds me of both Alex and Julian. Their type of humor is all different, but they all make me laugh. Or made me, in Alex's case. My chest fills with the now-familiar sadness, though it's a little more mellow each time.

Ranger: I've kissed this guy, and we've done frotting and hand jobs, but I'm ready to do more. Do I ask him? Tell him? Hint? What's the protocol here?

David: Any of the above will work. Or next time you see him, kiss him, put your hand on his dick, and say you'd love to taste him. I have yet to meet a man who will say no to that.

As always, David knows when to get serious. His timing has always been impeccable.

Ranger: OK. So no real protocol, is what you're saying.

David: No. It depends on how you guys communicate. Some men prefer to keep it subtle, and they'll hint and use nonverbal signals. Others want explicit consent, and they'll ask for it.

JULIAN IS SERIOUS ABOUT CONSENT, but I think the nonverbal thing would work with him. He's more worried about triggering me, I think, than about anything else. He's already made clear he's up for more.

Ranger: Thanks.

David: Feel free to text me a play-by-play later. Happy to review with you.

Ranger: SO not gonna happen.

David: Damn. Worth a try.

Just as I want to put my phone down and make myself some breakfast, it dings with an incoming message. It's Julian, texting a selfie of himself with Doc wearing a straw hat for some reason. They both look adorable.

Julian: Good morning. Did you sleep well?

I hesitate. I hate dumping my sads on him first thing in the morning, but it doesn't seem right to lie to him either.

Ranger: You two look cute.

Just when I'm convinced I've successfully evaded his question, Julian texts me back.

Julian: I'll take that as a no, then.

Ranger: Not really, no. Nightmare. Woke up around 3.

Julian: I'm so sorry. I hope you'll be able to get a nap in this afternoon.

People often think that "I'm sorry" is an empty cliché. It's not. I'd ten times rather hear that than have people try to fix my problems for me. I love it that Julian isn't giving me advice, telling me what to do. He's just with me in this, offering me support and nothing else.

Ranger: Thank you. I'm planning on it. Trying to find the energy now to make myself breakfast.

Julian: Want some company?

. . .

My immediate thought is to say no. I don't want him to see me so tired. It will take me a few hours to recover from this. But at the same time, the idea of seeing him makes my heart beat faster. I always feel better when he's around. I take a deep breath.

Ranger: Love some.

20

JULIAN

I debated with myself for ten minutes at the grocery store before finally deciding I was overthinking things. But now that I'm standing on Ranger's front porch with a bottle of orange juice and cheap champagne, it really does feel like too much. He invited me over for breakfast, not some fancy mimosa brunch.

Before I can run back to my truck and ditch the bag, he opens the front door. He looks tired, bags under his eyes and a slightly pale pallor to his skin, but the smile on his lips softens him.

"Morning," I say, awkwardly holding up the bag like a dork, wondering if I should greet him with a kiss or not. Ugh, why does *casual* always feel more fraught with ways to screw up?

"Morning." He seems just as unsure as I am, but he leans in for a quick kiss, then steps aside to motion me inside. "You didn't have to bring anything." He looks at the bags as he leads me to the kitchen, where Benny is waiting next to the stove, keeping an eye on things like a good boy.

"Oh, it's nothing. I stopped along the way to get stuff for mimosas. But if it's too much, or if you don't like mimosas... I'm not even sure if you drink alcohol. I know some people say it can make PTSD worse, so this was probably a really thoughtless thing for me to bring. We could just drink the orange juice sans alcohol, although I wasn't sure if you liked it with pulp or with—"

He gives me another kiss, this one harder and a little longer, his lips moving against mine until my nerves slowly slip away.

"A lot of alcohol can make PTSD worse, but one drink won't hurt anything. I'd love a mimosa."

"Great." I let out a long breath, determined to be less awkward for the rest of the morning, and pull the two bottles out of the bag to mix us a couple of drinks. "Breakfast smells delicious."

"It's nothing fancy, just pancakes and eggs," he says, sounding shy.

"Pancakes are my favorite. When I was a kid, my dad would make pancakes every Saturday morning. I would always wake up early to help him, and when he wasn't looking, I would pour chocolate chips into the batter. I felt so sneaky like I was getting away with something. It wasn't until I was a little older that it occurred to me that the chocolate chips always happened to be sitting out on the counter, and he always *just happened* to turn his back at the last minute to give me the perfect opportunity to dump some in." I smile at the memory.

"I don't think I have any chocolate chips." Ranger's shoulders slump.

I press a kiss to his cheek and hand him the drink I poured for him. "That's okay. Maybe next time." I don't want to *assume* that breakfast with him will be a regular occurrence, but I don't want him to feel bummed about not having chocolate chips either.

"Yeah, next time." Once he's finished cooking the food, we carry our plates to the table and sit down.

"So, um, do you want to talk about your nightmare?" I take a bite of my eggs and glance over at Benny lying on the floor next to Ranger's chair to avoid staring at Ranger and making him feel pressured or uncomfortable.

"Not really." He sounds tired all over again.

"That's fine," I assure him. "What should we talk about? I hate to say it, but I'm a bit rusty with breakfast conversation if you know what I mean."

He chuckles. "Yeah."

We eat in silence for a few minutes. The food is good. I'm not sure what Ranger has done with the eggs, but they're not bland and rubbery like most scrambled eggs are.

"So…I was thinking," he says as our plates are near empty. "Can I give you a blow job?"

You really should warn a guy before asking a question like that. I'm right in the middle of a sip of my mimosa when the question catches me off guard. I snort and sputter, the orange juice burning my nose as it spews out.

"Can we finish breakfast first?" I ask, grabbing a napkin and wiping my nose and mouth.

"Of course." He chews the last bite of his pancake. "That was too blunt, right? I texted my friend for advice, and he wasn't too specific. Although he did mention I should ask while we're kissing."

"That would've made it less surprising. But I can't say it's usually unwelcome to be offered a blow job, so that helped your case."

Ranger quirks his lips in a crooked smile. "Thank fuck for that."

I look down at my plate, suddenly not all that interested in finishing my food. "Well, I'm full."

He chuckles. "Good. Me too."

He takes both our plates and puts them in the sink while I stand up and hover uncertainly next to the table. "Bedroom?" I suggest, and he nods.

Luckily, as soon as the bedroom door shuts behind us, Ranger grabs me by the front of my shirt and drags me in for a kiss. His mouth against mine breaks up some of the awkward, anticipatory tension between us. A heated smolder starts deep in my belly and spreads through my body as he walks me backward toward the bed until my legs bump into it.

The hard steel of his erection nudges me as his tongue brushes against mine. His body feels more solid now than it did a couple of weeks ago. I slip my hands under his shirt, sliding them up until I find his nipple stud with my fingers. I roll it between my thumb and forefinger, then pluck his other nipple gently in the same way. His groan vibrates against my tongue, and he thrusts his hips against mine.

He runs his hands down and fumbles with unbuttoning my jeans. When the button pops free, he reaches into my briefs, palming my achingly hard cock. I nip at his lips, moaning as he wraps his fingers around me and strokes me slowly.

"I'm dying to taste you," he murmurs against my lips, and I gasp, nodding and bumping our noses together.

"Much better delivery," I praise with a smile against his mouth.

Hooking his fingers in the waist of my pants and underwear, Ranger shoves them down, letting them pool around my ankles, and then pushes me down onto the bed. I wrap a hand around the back of his neck and try to pull him along with me, but he breaks the kiss and drops to his knees.

Ranger looks so determined, kneeling between my legs, studying my cock like it's a test he needs to pass. I run my fingers through his hair gently, trying not to groan when he licks his lips, his hot breath puffing against the sensitive head of my erection.

"Tell me if I do it wrong?"

"As long as you don't use teeth, you can't do it wrong," I assure him with an encouraging smile.

He nods and leans forward, parting his lips just a little and pressing them to the head of my cock like he's giving it a kiss. A shiver runs through me, my erection twitching against his lips as my balls tighten. A quiet gasp falls from my lips, and I tighten my grasp on his short hair.

Ranger presses another kiss, a little farther down on my cock, catching a droplet of precum on his lips. He pulls back and licks it off his mouth, his eyes flashing with lust as he looks up at me. "Mmm." He hums, this time dragging the flat of his tongue over the head of my cock.

I whimper, more precum leaking out, which he laps up eagerly like it's the best thing he's tasted in his life. "Fuck," he mutters, kissing and licking the head of my cock the same way he always does with my mouth.

I try to spread my legs, but my pants around my ankles keep me from being able to. Every wet lap of his tongue sends sparks down my length, heating every inch of me from the inside out.

When he wraps his lips around me, I'm surprised I don't come on the spot. My cock jerks against the roof of his mouth as he slowly takes me deeper. Ranger looks up at me the entire time, his eyes fixed on mine, his lips red and stretched around my shaft.

He tries to take me deep but gags, his throat tightening around me in a way that makes me gasp again, more precum dripping onto his tongue as he sucks me in more shallow bobs this time. His technique is a bit sloppy, his rhythm inconsistent, but he makes up for it with an abundance of enthusiasm. He sucks me hard and fast, running his tongue along each throbbing vein as he sucks me hard and fast, and digging his fingers digging into my thighs. His grunts vibrate around my length.

"Ranger," I gasp his name, my hips twitching involuntarily. "I'm...oh...*ohhh*."

My body tenses, and my balls draw up tight. I try to shove his head away, but he only sucks me harder, looking more determined. When the first burst of my cum lands on his tongue, his eyes cloud with lust. He hums hungrily, lapping at the head of my cock as it pulses and fills his mouth with my hot, thick release.

He suckles me until my balls are sore and my cock is oversensitive before releasing me with a wet, sloppy *squelch*. I sag against the bed. The sound of his zipper echoes through the air as he undoes his own pants, yanks them down, and pulls out his hard cock.

"Fuck," he groans, working his hand furiously over his erection, his face pressed against the inside of my thigh. He kisses and bites my skin, grunting and groaning until a hard shudder runs through his body and cum shoots out of his cock and coats his hand and thighs.

I'm still catching my breath when Ranger climbs onto the bed, his cum streaked on his thighs and clinging to his softening cock.

"I'm wiped now. Take a nap with me?" he asks, yawning.

I nod and kick my pants off the rest of the way, then scoot up the bed and lay my head on the pillow next to his. He throws an arm around me and pulls me against his chest like I'm his favorite teddy bear. He's snoring in no time, and the slow, gentle rhythm of his breathing, along with the warmth of his body, drags me under as well.

21

RANGER

The *tsssskr* of the ice-cold can of Coke opening is music to my ears, and I guzzle down the first gulps. God, that tastes amazing. And I've burned more than enough calories the last two days to deserve this sugary treat.

I wipe down my face with a wet washcloth and plop down into one of the rocking chairs on my porch. I did it. Don't ask me where I got the energy and the motivation, but I painted the whole goddamn outside of the house in two days. The pale yellow looks stunning, although maybe a tad too happy and sunny for me, but whatever. It was the original color of the house, and I liked it.

It feels good to have accomplished something and even more to have checked such a big task off my to-do list. Granted, my body is cursing me because standing on a ladder apparently utilizes muscles that don't get much exercise otherwise, and my shoulders didn't appreciate me holding a brush for that long. But those are minor details.

What counts is that I'm proud of myself, and that's a feeling I haven't had in a while. I find myself smiling—in itself a rare occurrence. Unless I'm with Julian, who for some reason makes me happy all the time. Happy enough to sleep well. When he's with me at least. That nap I took, holding him in my arms, is the deepest I've slept in months.

I take out my phone, then hold it up at the right angle so it shows my naked chest, and take a picture.

Ranger: Need any more work done? I'm dressed for the occasion

Julian: Give me a second to wipe off my drool

I love how open and unashamed he is about what he likes. In this case, me. He's made no secret of the fact that my body turns him on, and it means something to me, though I don't want to dig too deep to find out why. Every man likes to hear he's attractive, I tell myself because obviously, that's why Julian's praise always makes me feel like I'm a better man than I think I am.

Julian: Sadly, no urgent handyman work available, but I'm happy to make something up if that means I get to stare at you working shirtless again...

My fingers already hover over the keyboard, but I change my mind. Every time we've met, it has been either here or at his house. And while I'd love to invite him to my place and show off my work, I'm worried about the message that will send. Look at me, painting the house! Sure, it's a monumental accomplishment for me, but it feels...weak.

It's not. Rationally, I know that. But a man has his pride. I don't want Julian to always see me as needing help, as vulnerable. He needs to discover that I've got skills too other than being able to fix a fence, wearing no shirt. I want to show him I've got skills, even if they're not obvious ones. So what can I do with him to share that other side of me?

I snap my fingers. That's it. The answer comes so quickly it's clearly the right choice. I can even argue that I'm doing it because I'm worried about him, not because of some stupid male pride.

Ranger: Pardon the abrupt segue, but have you ever shot a gun?

Julian: Erm, yeah. Once, way back, when my father had a flash of bonding need and took me to a shooting range. Can't say I remember much more than 'don't point at what you don't want to shoot.'

Ranger: Well, that's a great lesson to remember. Would you like me to teach you?

He's read my message but doesn't respond right away. Maybe I need to explain why? Not my reason, of course, but clarify that I want him safe.

Ranger: I was just thinking that you live there pretty isolated, so it might be good for you if you learned how to shoot so you can defend yourself if necessary. Not just from people but from animal attacks as well.

Julian: I don't mean to be insensitive, but are you sure it's a good idea for you? Won't it trigger you? I'm afraid you can't bring Benny. It would be way too loud for him.

How sweet of him to worry about that. It shows not only how much he knows about PTSD but also how much he cares about Benny *and* me.

Ranger: No, but thank you for checking. My triggers are unexpected sounds and movements. A shooting range is all expected actions. Plus, I'm the one shooting, so I'll be in control. And I'll have you with me...

Julian: Oh, okay. Good. In that case, I'd love to.

We set up a time for tomorrow, and I'm pretty damn proud of myself all over again as I put my phone away. "I've still got moves," I tell Benny, whose eyes betray nothing of the utter laughability he must feel about that statement. God bless dogs.

The next day, my muscles are slightly better. That yoga shit really does work, I'm telling you. It can't cure mental stuff, but it sure as fuck helps my body stay flexible and recover faster.

After a thorough shower in which I do a little manscaping, I opt for a good shave. Not that I want to presume, but should we progress to *pleasurable* activities of a more sexual nature, I want to be prepared. That's also why I put two condoms and a package of lube in my wallet. Thank god for Amazon Prime so I don't have to buy them in town.

I check myself in the mirror, and I'm startled by my own face. It's...different. Working outside has restored my tan, and my eyes don't have those awful bags underneath anymore. And I must've gained some weight because my cheeks have filled out a little. Damn, I look good, and warmth spreads through my chest.

When I arrive at the shooting range, I've barely gotten out of my truck when Julian pulls up beside me. My heart does a happy little jump I ignore. We're friends. With great benefits, but that's it. I'm not ready for more, and Julian sure wouldn't want something more with me anyway. He could do so much better.

"Hi," Julian says, and as if it's the most natural thing in the world, he steps toward me and presses a kiss on my lips.

I freeze, completely stunned. Not that I'm objecting, but I didn't think he'd want to be open about his...association with me.

"No PDAs, got it."

I shake my head to get out of this mental fog. "No! I mean, it's fine. I just wasn't expecting it. But it's fine. I promise. No harm done. All fine."

Julian's eyes twinkle. "That's a lot of 'fine' for one kiss."

I sigh, rolling my eyes at myself. "That's because it was a very fine kiss."

Julian's smile widens. "Good save."

We walk in together, and I sign him in as a guest after he's shown his driver's license to the receptionist. I'm a regular here. I've been a member for many years now. As an active military member and now a vet, I've never paid membership dues. I argued about that with the owner, but he insisted on it. Said it was the least he could do to thank me for my service. I don't know why, but that always makes me uncomfortable.

I give Julian a pair of ear protectors, then open my gun locker. I own several guns, some that are usually here and a few that I keep at home.

"This is a 9 mm handgun," I tell him, taking out my Sig Sauer P365. "It's a very popular handgun because it's relatively lightweight, so easy to use as a concealed carry."

I hand it to him after checking it's empty.

He holds it, weighing it in his hand. "It's much lighter than I'd expected."

"It'll be heavier when it's loaded, obviously, but for someone like you, that would be a good choice to use."

"Are we using this one to practice with?"

"Yes, but I also want to let you feel the difference with a heavier gun."

I replace the Sig Sauer with my Magnum .45. "This one's so much heavier," Julian says.

"It is, and that makes it much harder to shoot for a rookie. It has a vicious kickback that isn't easy to control at first."

"Is that the heaviest gun you have?"

"No. At home, I have a 50 caliber Desert Eagle. It's a great gun, but only for experienced gunmen."

We make our way onto the range, me carrying the Sig Sauer and the .45.

"Your dad probably gave you the safety instructions, but I'd be remiss if I didn't talk about them with you."

Julian nods. He's focused, and I like that he takes this as seriously as I do. I love guns, but they're no joke and not something to play with lightly. So I run him through ten minutes of safety drills, teaching him to keep his finger off the trigger, never point the gun, and how to safely check if it's loaded. We practice taking the magazine out, loading it, and then making sure it's placed correctly.

After he's done it a few times, it's time to have some fun.

"What do I aim for?" Julian asks.

My mouth twitches.

"Yeah, yeah, I've seen the big black target, but how do I aim?"

"Always aim for the chest because it's the biggest area. If you miss, chances are you'll hit something else important."

"Okay."

He's adorably concentrated as he takes aim and fires. His shot is over by quite a bit, and he looks disappointed. "Don't hold your breath and relax your shoulders," I advise.

His second shot is closer, though still a miss.

"You need to gently squeeze the trigger rather than pull it. Pulling it will cause your gun to go upward slightly, and you'll miss your target."

He nods and takes a stand again, more relaxed this time. His fourth shot hits. It's far off from the center, but Julian is all but jumping up and down. "That was good, right?"

"Yup, you hit something. Try again."

After twenty bullets, he's getting tired. His hands are shaking, and I gently take the gun from him. "That was fun." Julian smiles from ear to ear. "Show me what you can do."

"It's not a competition. That wouldn't be fair to you. I did this for a living."

He rolls his eyes at me. "Duh, silly. I know that. I just want to see how good you are...if you want to."

Do I want to? When he asks it like that, his expression eager and honest, hell yes, I do. I reload the gun, then take a stand and fire in rapid succession. I don't need to check the target to know I've hit dead center on all of them, but Julian's open mouth and bulging eyes are balm to my wounded soul. I take off my ear protectors.

"That's amazing," he says. "That's... You didn't even look, it seemed."

"It's muscle memory by now. I've done this so many times, with so many different guns, ranging from rifles to semi-automatic guns to old-fashioned revolvers. There's not a gun in the world I can't shoot."

Pride rings in my voice, but Julian doesn't take offense at it. Instead, he sends me a blinding smile filled with something else I can't quite put my finger on, but it looks like admiration. "I'm genuinely impressed."

My chest feels like butterflies have taken up residence there, and while it's a completely unfamiliar sensation, I like it. "Do you still want to try the Magnum?" I ask.

"At least once. I'm curious about that kickback."

I run him through the correct posture, warning him not to lock his arm as he fires. He takes a long time, then pulls the trigger, and I can all but see him gather the courage. The effect is what I expected: as soon as he's fired, his hands fly upward, and despite him holding the gun with two hands, he almost drops it. "Holy gumballs! You warned me, and I still wasn't ready..."

"Don't blame yourself. Like I said, this is not a gun for beginners..."

He's peppering me with questions as we get back to my locker, where I check all the guns, do a quick clean, then store them. He's so curious, unafraid to ask what others might consider stupid questions. I don't think they are, don't get me wrong. Of course they're beginner questions, but that's fine. We all have to start somewhere, and showing him just a little of what I'm highly skilled at makes me feel *good* inside. Really, really good.

As we walk back into the parking lot, Julian puts a hand on my arm. "If there's a smooth segue to go from shooting a gun to inviting you over for entirely different activities, I couldn't think of it, and I'm telling you I tried hard. So we'll go with the old-fashioned direct approach. Wanna come home with me? Watching you shoot has made me want to climb you…"

22

JULIAN

I've always considered myself to be a pacifist. I didn't want to burst Ranger's bubble when he suggested that he wanted to teach me to defend myself, but I'd sooner let a bear maul me than shoot at it. I have to admit, though, that target practice was fun. And more than that, it was unbelievably sexy to see Ranger in his element, his face full of pride, his muscles flexing... Whew, it's making my dick hard just thinking about it.

Since we arrived at the range separately, he follows me in his truck back to my place and parks next to me. For just a second as I make my way from my truck to the house, I notice the red hue of the sky from the wildfires. I make a mental note to check how far off they are now. The smell of burning wood seems heavier.

"Do you want something to drink?" I ask as we both kick off our shoes. Princess Pinecone greets us with a tail wag, nudging my hand with her snout until I give her a scratch behind her ears.

"Water's fine."

"Coming right up. Make yourself comfortable." I head

into the kitchen to get a couple of glasses of water. When I return to the living room, I catch Ranger stretching his neck and using his fingers to knead the muscles.

"Are you okay?" I set down the glasses and sit next to him on the couch.

"I'm fine, just a little sore. I spent the past few days painting my house, basically sending my body into shock with the sudden bout of activity," he says, shooting me a wry smile. "Yoga and a shower this morning loosened them up a bit, but then the shooting made me tense all over again."

"If you want, I could give you a massage," I offer, waggling my eyebrows. "I have oils and everything."

"Really?" He perks up.

"I give *excellent* massages," I purr. Okay, more often than not, I'm massaging the horses, but they never complain, and let me tell you, horses are *much* harsher critics than humans, so I'm pretty confident in my skills. Besides, any excuse I can come up with to get this man shirtless and oiled up is a win in my book.

"I'd love a massage," Ranger agrees.

I take his hand, thread my fingers through his, and yank him off the couch. "I'll go get the oils. You get shirtless and go lie on my bed." I point him in the direction of my bedroom and give him a playful slap on the ass, which earns me an arched eyebrow. I chuckle and make a shooing motion, taking a second to appreciate the way his jeans hug his ass as he heads toward my bedroom. "Lose the jeans too," I call after him.

"I'm starting to think this massage idea is just an excuse to get me naked."

I gasp with feigned indignation. "I would *never*."

The rich sound of his laugh echoes down the hall, sending a happy little thrill through me.

With my oils in hand, I bite back a groan as I step into my bedroom. The sight of Ranger in nothing but a pair of tight black briefs, spread out facedown on my bed, is the stuff wet dreams are made of. Dark hair covers his thighs, which are widened just a little but oh-so inviting. I wonder how he would feel about my tongue on his hole. He said he was up for a bit of exploration, but rimming is over the line for a lot of men. I palm my cock and give myself just one second to indulge in the fantasy of grabbing Ranger's cheeks and stroking him with my tongue until he's screaming with pleasure.

I let out a long breath through my nose and climb onto the bed, then shuffle up until I'm straddling his glorious, glorious ass. I can't resist giving one of the cheeks a quick slap just to watch it jiggle.

"Hey," he protests with another laugh.

"Sorry, I was compelled by the God of Glorious Glutes." I shrug, even though his face is buried in my pillow. Ungh, to have him biting that pillow. Focus, Julian, focus. Massage first...okay, massage with a side of seduction, *then* fun.

As I click open the cap on the oil, the soothing scent of lavender fills the room. I pour a generous amount into my palms and rub them together to get the oil nice and warm, then lay my hands on his shoulders and knead his tight muscles.

Ranger gives a low moan. "Smells good," he mumbles into the pillow.

"Lavender is great for stress relief." At least it is in horses, so probably humans too.

I put my muscles into working out a big knot right between his shoulder blades. The oil warms a bit more against his skin, helping my hands to slide easily. Ranger relaxes little by little, letting me knead his muscles into submission until he's like melted butter underneath me.

My cock is more than half-hard, pressing against the curve of his ass, and every one of his muffled groans makes me harder. Honestly, I should earn some kind of medal of honor for not grinding myself against him.

I shimmy down a little so I can work on his lower back. "If you want, you can take your underwear off so I don't get them all oily," I say oh-so innocently. Ranger rumbles with amusement. I'm not fooling him for a second.

"If I do, are you going to spank me again?"

I tsk. "Please, I am a *professional*."

"Uh-huh." He doesn't seem terribly convinced, but he hooks his thumbs in the waistband of his briefs anyway and shoves them down.

Sweet baby unicorns. Ungh.

I lean over and bite the plump globe of his behind. Ranger squeals in a very dignified, armed forces sort of way.

"A bite is not a spank," I point out before he can accuse me of breaking my word.

He mutters something that sounds like *semantics*, and I return to massaging him. I press my hands over his lower back and then slowly down to his butt, which seems as tense as the rest of him. He should work on unclenching from time to time. I guess that's what I'm here to help him with.

I knead his butt muscles harder, shamelessly parting them just enough to get a peek at his hole. My cock jerks, precum dampening my underwear, and I bite back a groan.

"Where do you stand on butt stuff?" I ask, my voice coming out strained, not as casual as I was hoping for.

"Butt stuff? Are we twelve?" His voice drips with amusement, but I notice he tilts his hips up just a little, maybe subconsciously?

"My finger in your ass," I say bluntly. "Possibly my tongue. Maybe one day, my cock if you're interested."

Ranger tightens his arms around the pillow, his hips jerking and his hole clenching and then relaxing.

"Okay," he answers roughly.

"Okay?" What exactly is he agreeing to? Specifics are good in these situations.

"Maybe just your fingers today so we can see how that goes."

I grunt in agreement, kneading his muscles deeper, then slipping one thumb into the crease of his cheeks and just barely teasing his hole. Ranger lies perfectly still, seeming to hold his breath as I grab the bottle of oil again and drizzle some into his crease, then use two fingers to spread it around the outside of his hole.

Using my index and middle finger, I gently circle his rim, waking up all those nerve endings he probably never knew he had. Back and forth, round and round, just like I'd do with my tongue, slowly coaxing him to relax for me.

"You're so sexy," I murmur, leaning forward and kissing his oiled shoulder. "I'm kind of crazy about you," I confess, hoping he won't read more into the words than is safe. I don't want to scare him away, but my mouth seems to be running away with me.

His hole softens enough that a bit of pressure lets the tip of my finger ease inside. He gasps and clenches, and I press another series of kisses against his back, down his spine, whispering more sweet words I hope he's too lust drunk to pay much attention to.

Ranger's inner muscles are tight, his channel hot and silky as I gradually push my finger inside, little by little until I'm knuckle deep.

I take it slow at first, gently stroking my finger in and out, using my thumb to tease the rim of his hole between thrusts. With my free hand, I trail along his back, over his ass, down his thighs, gathering every grunt and gasp he gives me and storing them away to think about later, over and over.

I add a second finger and fuck him faster. I crook my digits in search of his prostate, my cock throbbing when he lets out a sharp gasp and pushes himself back against my fingers. "Oh god, that's..."

I dig my other fingers into his butt cheek and peg his prostate again and again until he's a panting and trembling mess.

"Oh fuck. Oh, god. Julian." Ranger cants his hips helplessly, fucking himself on my fingers, his fists clenched tightly around my bedsheets. A shudder runs through his body, and his inner muscles clamp tightly around my fingers. Another low, long groan falls from his lips, making my cock ache and my balls tighten.

I work my fingers in and out, fucking him through his orgasm until he collapses back onto the bed with a tired sigh.

I hastily unbutton my pants, shove them down just enough to reach one oily hand inside, and pull out my cock. I'm already throbbing desperately, right on the edge after Ranger's ass pulsed around my fingers.

I ease my fingers out of his now relaxed hole, glistening with oil, and grab his cheek and spread as I fist my cock.

"Ranger..." I gasp his name, and he groans in response. My hand flies over my erection, tugging hard and fast as I imagine how good it would feel to sink inside him and fill him with my cum. "Ungh," I cry out, my balls tightening and my cock spasming in my grasp.

Hot, thick ropes of cum shoot out, covering Ranger's

hole, landing across the swell of his ass cheeks, dripping into his crease. I pant and moan, slowing my strokes but unwilling to stop staring at how perfectly debauched Ranger looks covered in my release.

I shuffle off him and get a towel to clean him up. Even if it should be illegal to clean up such a pretty, pretty mess.

"Wait," he grunts.

"I'm going to get a towel."

"Come here first." I crawl back up the bed and lie down next to him. He lifts his arm and drapes it over me, a smile on his lips, his face looking thoroughly relaxed, which I take as evidence of a job well done. "I'm a little crazy about you too," he says. My heart leaps into my throat. Before I can try to backtrack or reassure him I didn't mean anything serious by it, he presses a soft kiss to my lips. "Lie here for a few minutes. Then we'll shower together again. I liked that."

"I liked that too." I kiss him one more time, then rest my forehead against his, closing my eyes, and sink into the moment while it lasts.

23

RANGER

"What does it mean when a guy tells you he's kind of crazy about you?" I blurt out as soon as Lucky picks up. I've only been contemplating that very question for the last forty-eight hours, trying to play it cool with Julian while at the same time panicking every time I think about him.

I hear someone talk in the background. "It's Ranger. Go back to sleep, Mase," Lucky says softly, and I can hear him walk away.

Oops. I cringe. Guess I should've checked the time before I called him at seven in the morning on a Saturday. In my defense, I've been awake for two hours already. Apparently, that's what happens when you go to sleep at nine. Who fucking knew? I've done my yoga routine, greeting the sun and all that crap, and I've even had breakfast already. Major points for adulting today.

"I love you, but why the everloving fuck are you calling me at the ass crack of dawn to talk about your love life?" Lucky mutters, still sounding like he's half-asleep. That won't last long. We're the same: instantly awake. "You couldn't wait until a more godly hour? What are you doing up anyway?"

"Sorry? I forgot to check the time."

"Are you okay?" Lucky's voice is sharp now, and I feel awful.

"I am. I'm sorry. I wasn't thinking. Want me to call back later?"

He scoffs. "Like I could fall asleep again now. I'm already making coffee, so spill."

"I've been sleeping better...getting up earlier as a result."

"That's great, but not the kind of spilling I meant. Who said he was kind of crazy about you? When did it happen, and why is it a problem?"

Calling my brother was a spectacularly bad idea, wasn't it? I'm never gonna hear the end of this. What the fuck was I thinking? "Julian." I resign myself to the inevitable.

"Ah. You took my advice about having some casual fun with him."

"Yes."

"And was that statement uttered with a clear state of mind, or can you attribute it to the throes of passion?"

I snort. "Have you been reading romances again?"

"I'll have you know I'm intimately familiar with the throes of passion. In fact, last night we—"

"Yeah, yeah. I believe you. Don't need details, man."

"Damn. Just when I was about to give you a play-by-play..."

I shudder, even though I know damn well he's messing with me. "Can we focus on me again?"

"You haven't answered my question."

Right. The throes of passion. "I don't think it qualified."

"Want me to make sure? Just say the word...all the

words, in specific detail. This is one area where I won't mind you being long-winded."

God, he's such an ass. But I don't know who else to ask. "He was giving me a massage."

"With a happy ending?"

I think back on the unforgettable feeling of Julian's fingers in my hole, electrifying my spine, my balls, my dick. Some of the details are a little hazy. It was impossible to pay proper attention, what with him leading me straight to paradise's door, but I'm pretty sure I shamelessly fucked myself on his fingers. Hello, prostate, nice to meet you. I clear my throat. "A *very* happy ending."

"Was it good?"

"Yeah."

"And he told you he liked you."

"He said he was kind of crazy about me…and I said I was a little crazy about him as well. And now I'm wondering what that meant and what the fuck is happening here."

"It sounds to me like he genuinely likes you." Lucky's tone has changed, all the teasing gone.

The panic is back in full force. "What does that mean? This was supposed to be casual, fun. I told him I wasn't ready for a relationship, for anything serious."

"Mack, he *likes* you. It's the same as when a girl or a woman told you she liked you."

I feel like a complete moron. "I'm… That hasn't happened to me since high school, so forgive me if my memory is a little foggy."

"Do you like him?"

My mouth curls up in a smile of its own volition. Just thinking of Julian makes me…happy. He's funny and positive, encouraging and inspiring. And I love how he's so open in expressing his appreciation of my body and me as a person. He makes me want to do better, try harder.

"I do."

"One sec." A coffee machine bubbles and sputters, then the unmistakable sound of fluid dripping into a cup. "Finally. Coffee," Lucky says with a sigh, and we're both quiet for a few beats.

"Do you feel guilty?" he finally asks.

I've wondered that myself. It's the most obvious explanation, isn't it? That I'd experience guilt toward Alex. But that's not it. It's more that I feel so woefully unready for anything serious, as damaged and incomplete as I am. Julian deserves better. "I don't think I do. He and I were never together, so it's not like I'm betraying him."

"But you loved him. Even if it never came to anything, you loved him. Maybe subconsciously it makes you guilty to move on so quickly?"

Frowning, I walk out the front door and sit on the rocking chair on the porch, Benny by my side. He's alert, clearly picking up on my stress, and I rub his head. But it seems he's only half-assured. He sits down next to me but doesn't lie at my feet. He's keeping an eye on me, and it's the best thing in the world.

Why is Lucky arguing this point with me? "It's been a year. Is that really so quickly? Besides, even if Julian likes me and I enjoy spending time with him, that doesn't mean we're in a serious relationship."

"But you're getting there."

"So what?" I snap. "Don't I deserve some fucking happiness?"

And then it hits me. Fucking asshole is doing what he always did best: playing devil's advocate.

"You do, bro, and it's time you fully accept that as well. If being with Julian brings you joy, then embrace that, regardless of where it leads. You deserve to be happy, so allow yourself to feel it..."

I'm just about to answer him when I spot something in the distance. Smoke. I hadn't noticed it before as the sun was still rising, but it's unmistakable now. I sniff the air, and the burning scent tickles my nose. How close has that forest fire gotten? My heart skips a beat. Julian.

"Hold on," I tell Lucky as I quickly pull up the app that shows all the fires. I zoom in, and my heart jumps into overdrive. It's right on his doorstep. "I need to go."

"Mack, I'm sorry if—"

"No, it's not that. The Segura fire... It's only miles away from Julian now. He—"

"Go. We'll talk later. Go!"

I end the call, then immediately call Julian. I'm already out the door, grabbing the bag I packed days ago just in case. It's got precious little: some clothes, Alex's letter and things, one photo album, my uniform, and my medals. I don't care about anything else.

Julian picks up within seconds. "It's...it's bad." he says, his voice breaking. "The wind changed direction overnight. We just got the order to evacuate. I don't know what to do."

"I'm on my way."

24

JULIAN

I bought this property five years ago, and each wildfire season, I've counted my lucky stars that it's remained unscathed. Apparently, my luck has finally run out. The sky is dark, smoke blocking out the sun. Sirens wail in the distance. The stench of everything burning is so thick my throat aches, and my eyes burn. The order to evacuate came through about twenty or so minutes ago, and I've been panicking ever since.

Princess Pinecone whines, pressing her head against my thigh and panting anxiously.

"I know, babe. I'm working on a plan." Not that there's much to *plan* for. We got an evacuation order, which means we need to get the fuck out of here. No time for cutesy expressions or anything fun. We're fucked. "Okay, we can do this." I feign confidence, although I'm frozen to the spot as I try not to have a panic attack.

My brain is throwing a dozen suggestions at me all at once: get PP in the truck and hightail it out of here, hook up the trailer and load up the rest of the animals, figure out where Butler ran off to after breaking down his fence *again*...

Is curling into a ball and flat out hyperventilating an option? Because that's about where I'm at.

Like an angel sent to answer my prayers, Ranger's truck rolls into my driveway just as I'm about to fall to pieces. He throws the thing into Park, then jumps out, leaving Benny, panting as anxiously as PP is, in the cab.

"J, are you okay?" He rushes over to me in long, steady strides, his shoulders squared, and his face etched with a calm authority I've never seen there before. "Breathe," he says firmly, putting his hands on my shoulders as soon as he's in front of me.

I drag in a deep breath, the heavy scent of smoke filling my nostrils and making my heart flail even more wildly, the animal part of my brain screaming at me that there's danger.

"I don't know what to do," I mutter helplessly, looking out over my fields. The eerie glow of the approaching fire lights up the sky, which grows darker with smoke by the minute.

"I'm running point. Got it?" he says, and I bob my head in agreement, relief washing over me at the fact that he's level-headed enough to take control right now. "I'll put PP into my car. Did you pack like I told you to last week?"

I nod numbly. When the fires started getting closer, Ranger told me to have a "go-bag" ready in case we needed to leave without prep time. I shoved a few handfuls of clothes into a bag, a photo album, important documents, and general irreplaceables.

"My animals." Again, I desperately glance at my field, where my horses are pacing, tossing their heads, neighing loudly.

"We have to turn them loose. I know it sucks, but it's

their best chance at survival. We'll never get them all loaded into a trailer in time."

"I can't leave Doc." I don't want to leave any of my animals, but there's no way Doc would make it on his own. The horses have a chance, albeit a slim one. And Butler's already taken his survival into his own hands by running off, whether I like it or not. But I can bring Doc. "And my chickens." They won't make it either. The smoke is already too much for them, and they'll never outrun the fire if it makes it here.

"Fuck," Ranger mutters. "Okay, you have a trailer for him?" I point toward the side of the barn where I keep the small horse trailer. "Grab your stuff. I'll hook up the trailer, and then we'll *try* to get Doc. If he won't cooperate, though, I'm sorry we'll have to leave him."

My heart squeezes, but I nod. It only takes me a second to get PP into Ranger's truck, meeting an exciting Benny. Then I run inside to grab my bag. Everything else I leave behind with a silent prayer the house will make it.

When I get back outside, Ranger has the trailer hooked up. I toss my stuff into the cab of my truck and then haul ass to open all the gates. The horses are worked up enough that they take off immediately. Tears spring into my eyes, and I can hardly breathe not just from the thick air but also from not knowing whether I'll see my horses again.

The girls are next. They flap wildly and wiggle in my arms as I carry them two at a time out to the truck. I always have a dog kennel strapped down in the bed of the truck in case of an emergency. I toss Dorothy and Blanche inside, then go back for Rose and Sophia, the latter pecking at me aggressively.

When I rush into the barn, Doc is snorting and pacing inside his stall, banging against the gate frantically. There's no way I'll be able to get a harness on him, so I'm hoping he'll cooperate and run straight into the trailer just outside the barn entrance. I cross my fingers and throw open his gate. He brays and gallops past me. I let out a sigh of relief when I hear the thunderous echo of his hooves on the trailer ramp.

I grab his harness and lead rope off the wall and sprint out of the barn. Ranger is closing up the trailer with my donkey inside.

"Where are we going? Your place?"

"Can't. We haven't been given official orders to evacuate yet, but they said on the radio when I was driving over that it's likely coming for my county in the next few hours. Let's head a few hours north and find somewhere to stay for the night. Follow me. You have your cell in case we lose each other?"

I pat my pockets until I find it. "I've got it."

"Good. Let's get going."

He turns, but I grab his shirt to stop him, pressing a fast but hard kiss to his lips. "Thank you. You saved the day."

"I'm not good for much, but staying level-headed in a crisis is one area I excel in."

If I were in any frame of mind to flirt right now, I'd tell him he seems to be good at plenty of things. As it stands, I let him usher me to the driver's side of my truck. He opens the door and helps me inside.

"Drive safely," he says firmly.

"Yes, *Ranger*," I emphasize his name, his *title* he's very much living up to in this moment.

I follow his truck in a bit of a daze, glancing into my rearview mirror frequently to see the wildfire. It's both a relief and the strange feeling of missing a step when it's no longer visible. I know we're getting farther away, going somewhere safe, but it's as if the danger exists in a completely different universe. I just drove away from my home, from all the things, all the living creatures that mean the most to me, and I have no idea if I'll ever see them again. Something tells me I shouldn't hold my breath for it.

I'm not even sure what city we're in when Ranger pulls off the highway two hours later, but I follow him blindly. He turns into the parking lot of a motel. It's empty enough that there's plenty of room to park my trailer.

Ranger gets out of his truck. PP jumps out as well and barrels past him, while Benny politely waits like a good boy. At least *he's* proof I'm a decent trainer.

I sag against the side of my truck, squatting down as PP reaches me and wrapping her in a hug. She presses her head against my chest, her way of hugging me back, and wags her tail.

"I'm going to go check us into a room. I'll be right back."

"Thanks," I say, the word muffled by PP's fur. Doc brays loudly as Ranger walks away, and I give my dog one more kiss on the head, then stand up and peek through the slats of the trailer. He looks like he's doing fine, but I need to get him water as soon as possible.

Ranger comes back a few minutes later, a room key clutched in his hand.

"We've got the room at the very end." He points at the last door.

"That's perfect. I'll pull the trailer around to the side of the building there. I need to find some water for Doc, and then once it's dark, we can sneak him into the room."

"I'm sorry. We can *what* now?"

25

RANGER

I stare at Julian. No way in hell did he just suggest we put a donkey and four chickens in our motel room.

He crosses his arms. "We'll sneak them into the room once it's dark."

"Julian..."

"Doc can't stay by himself in the trailer. He'll go crazy with loneliness. He's a people person...a people animal. Whatever. Besides, someone could steal him."

Incredulity fills my voice. "You think someone would steal a deaf donkey?"

"They might, and I won't let that happen."

"And you think people will steal chickens as well?"

He stares at me as if I just said the stupidest thing. "Duh. They'll take them and eat them."

"I'm not sure there are that many people left who can kill and skin a chicken."

"And I don't intend to find out if any of them live in this town. The animals are coming inside."

I must be more fucked up than I realized before because bossy Julian is incredibly hot. The way he puts his hands on his hips, his eyes spewing fire and his mouth set in an adorably stubborn way makes me want to jump him. The fact that a donkey and four chickens will be watching is enough to douse that particular desire quickly, though.

I drag a hand through my hair, though I know I already lost this fight. "Those chickens will wreck the room. They'll poop everywhere."

Julian shrugs. "We'll put a tarp on the floor, create a coop for them."

It's clear I don't stand a chance, and I surrender to the inevitable. "We passed a Walmart Supercenter on the way into town. I'll head over and get us the supplies we need."

Julian smiles at me, his eyes tired and showing his worry and stress. "Thank you. For everything."

I lean in and kiss him softly on his lips. "No thanks needed. Go get some water for Doc, and I'll be back as quickly as I can."

The sky is dark and eerily red, even here, a hundred miles away from the fire, and the faint smell of smoke tinges the air. The wind is in this direction, and even though it's the middle of the day, it feels like it's dusk. I turn on the radio as I drive off the motel's parking lot.

"...and more firefighters have flown in from across the nation to help out. Two teams from Canada and a Mexican firefighters crew have arrived as well. The strong wind overnight made the Segura fire—which had been seventy percent contained—pick up in intensity again, roaring across hundreds of acres within hours. Local officials are urging the last residents to evacuate immediately, as they don't expect to be able to hold off the fire much longer from destroying the town."

I wince, but at the same time, deep gratitude fills me that we were able to get out in time. Julian is safe, and that's what matters most. It'll be a hard hit for him to lose his farm, but we can rebuild that. Money matters, of course it does, but in the end, it's only money. I do hope and pray his horses will find a way out, but they're super smart animals with a strong survival instinct, so my hope is not unfounded.

Once we've arrived at Walmart, I let Benny out of the truck. He licks my hand, and I crouch down and rub his head. "I'm okay, buddy. Tired and worried, but I'm okay. Thank you for checking on me."

We walk in, Benny close by my side, and I don't dally as I grab what we need. A couple of cases of water. Boxes of meal bars and some other snacks. Tarp, rope, straw, and god bless them, they have chicken wire, so I get a roll of that as well. The room had a desk, so we can put them under there and create a coop with the wire.

I also get us some microwave meals. Everyone always bitches about how disgusting those things are, but once you've lived for weeks on freeze-dried food and MREs, those dinners are Michelin star-worthy.

Now I need food for Doc and the chickens. What the hell do chickens eat? I use my phone to do a quick Google search. Walmart doesn't sell actual chicken feed, but apparently, they'll eat vegetable peels, all kinds of fruits, corn, and more. That's doable.

What about Doc? Thank fuck for good cell signal because once again, my phone comes in handy. Whole grain bread works, and fruit and veggies. Okay, then. I get enough veggies to feed an army of chickens and donkeys and hurry to the register.

Those self-scan checkouts are the best invention since the microwave. Not only do they go way faster than regular checkouts, but it also means I don't have to talk to other people. It only takes me a few minutes to scan everything, and then I'm out the door. On the way back, I listen to the radio again, and the news is bad. For now, my house is safe, but it doesn't look good for Julian's.

When I get back to the motel, Julian has found a perfect spot to park the trailer. He's inside, holding up the water-filled ice bucket from our room for Doc, who's eyeing it suspiciously, then takes a tentative lap.

"Why isn't he drinking?" I ask.

"Donkeys are notoriously fussy about drinking. They refuse to drink if the water isn't clean or if the bucket or trough they're drinking from is dirty. Must be some evolutionary survival instinct."

And I learned something new again. I love watching Julian with his animals. He treats them like people, talking to them and constantly interacting. It's endearing.

"I've got us a bunch of supplies, so I'm gonna set up a chicken coop." I inspect the donkey again. "I'm still not sure about Doc, but we'll see."

Half an hour later, I've created a construction under the desk that should hold the chickens for at least a day or two. A double layer of tarp on the floor, a comfortable bed of straw, and the chicken wire fastened to the four desk legs. The provisional coop is still open on one end so we can put the chickens in, but I've got tie wraps to secure it. Tie wraps and duct tape—every handyman's go-to tools.

"That's perfect," Julian says as he inspects my creative solution. Warmth fills my chest at the idea of being useful again. Then Julian walks up to me and hugs me tightly, his arms holding me as if he doesn't intend to let go. "Thank you. I'm so, so happy you're here with me. I would've been lost without you."

The light inside me spreads, and it settles deep into my soul, where it chips away at the darkness that's slowly getting defeated. I press my cheek against Julian's soft hair, breathing in his smell. "There's nowhere I would rather be right now than here with you," I say, and I mean every fucking word.

He finally lets go. His eyes are suspiciously moist as he clears his throat. "I just checked the status of the fire again... and it's not good."

My heart hurts for him. "I know. I listened to the radio."

"My ranch... I don't think it'll survive."

"It doesn't look good."

"What will I do? With my chickens and Doc and Butler, and hopefully my horses, where can I go? It's not like I can just move in somewhere temporarily."

To hear him so dejected gnaws at my insides. It's so unlike him, and I want to do everything in my power to fix this for him. "I don't know, but we'll figure it out. You're not alone."

I hold my breath after that last statement. That's a big declaration from someone who insisted on keeping it casual.

But he sends me a sad smile. "Thank you. You have no idea how much that means to me."

Honestly, when he looks at me like that, he could tell me we'd need to put the four chickens, the donkey, the goat, and his horses in the room, plus our two dogs, and I'd still say yes.

26

JULIAN

Once we get Doc and the girls into the room, I flop down onto the bed with a relieved sigh. PP and Benny are lying at the foot of the bed, eyeing the menagerie skeptically, both throwing me occasional looks that clearly ask if I'm aware there's a donkey inside.

I should check my insurance policy to find out exactly how boned I am if I get back to a house that isn't there. My horses are all insured separately, since they're my business, but that's not much comfort. Sure, I'll get a payout to buy new horses, but that won't replace the ones I've lost. Getting a new horse to train won't fill the void left by Dino's sense of humor and wild spirit or Raleigh's utter obsession with apples to the point that he'll chew a hole right through my pocket to get to them if need be. I braided Bella's tail yesterday. Will it be the last time?

My chest aches just thinking about them.

Right now, there's nothing I can do about Butler, my horses, or my house. That's all up to fate, but at least I have Doc, PP, and my chickens safe and sound with me. Ranger didn't mean anything by it, but when he suggested we leave them outside for the night, I just about had another panic attack. With everything else so uncertain tonight, I need to know without a shadow of a doubt that at least some of my babies are okay.

Doc saunters over and noses at the bed like he might clamber on with the rest of us. He swings his tail from side to side, tugging at the sheets with his teeth.

"No," Ranger says and signs at the same time. "I can live with a donkey in the room, but I draw the line at sharing a bed." The authority in his tone is hot, even in a stressful situation like this. Actually, it might be *hotter* in a stressful situation like this. I was on the verge of falling apart earlier. I'm still not holding it together all that well, but it feels like he has this handled, and that's the most comforting thing I could imagine right now. Aside from my chickens. They're pretty comforting too.

Doc draws his ears back and brays at him, clearly not impressed by the boundaries Ranger gave him. But after a stern look from Ranger, he snorts and lies down on the floor instead. Yup, the man is ridiculously attractive when he's in charge. I'll have to remember that for later. Would he be into role-play?

"You learned sign language?" I roll onto my side and face Ranger, who's now climbing onto the other side of the bed.

"Just a few things so I could talk to Doc properly."

My heart flutters, a smile stretching over my lips. He built a makeshift chicken coop in our motel room, he learned sign language for my deaf donkey...he's *really* not making it easy not to fall for him.

"Have you checked in with your brother? He's safe in LA, right?" I check, scooting a little closer and laying my head against Ranger's chest. As soon as I do it, I realize it might be a bit much, but he doesn't complain. Quite the opposite, in fact. He slowly runs his fingers through my hair, soothing me with the hypnotic motion. I hum contentedly, letting my eyelids droop closed.

"He's okay. The fire's to the east, heading for our houses, but there's nothing more than smoke in LA."

"Good. I'm happy he's safe."

"You don't even know him." He sounds amused, but his voice is soft, like the cuddling is relaxing him as much as it does me.

"I don't need to know someone to be happy they're safe." I shrug.

His fingers stop moving in my hair for a second, his whole body falling still before there's a gentle press against the top of my head. His lips. My heart gives another one of those stupid, happy jolts, which I won't feel bad about. I have enough to worry about right now without getting myself all in a tizzy about the fact that my feelings for Ranger are far from casual. If I'm being honest with myself, I'm not sure they weren't all that casual to begin with.

I tilt my head back so I can see his face and bring my hand up to his cheek. There's a little bit of prickly stubble on his cheeks that abrades my fingertips as I drag them against the grain and then back the other way. He leans into my touch and presses a kiss to my palm when my hand comes near his lips. Ranger's gaze meets mine, and an electric current passes between us. Does he feel it too?

"I have to tell you something." The moment feels too fragile for anything but whispers. Part of me thinks I should keep my mouth shut. My house is probably burning to the ground as we speak. The last thing I need to do is set our relationship, or rather, our *arrangement* on fire too. But maybe that's just it. I need something stable under my feet with so much uncertainty swirling around me, and if Ranger can't be that, it's better to know right now.

"Tell me." He speaks just as softly, still stroking my hair with one hand, the other finding its way onto my hip and slipping under my shirt. His strong, steady fingers feel good against my skin, safe and exciting all at once. I desperately want more, but not just physically, and that's where this conversation comes in.

"I'm messing up this whole casual thing," I confess.

He frowns, his forehead wrinkling. "What do you mean?"

"I like you too much. I want more, even though I know it's not fair to ask you that after you made your feelings on the subject clear."

His breath hitches, and his body tenses for a second. Yup, I ruined everything. Benny whines and crawls up the bed enough to nose Ranger's elbow. He takes his hand off my belly and sinks his fingers into the dog's fur, closing his eyes for a moment until his jaw unclenches.

"Can I have a minute?" he asks, his voice strained.

I sit up and scoot away from him, guilt and humiliation warring inside me. Why did I have to open my mouth? Couldn't I have waited until we got back home so he won't have to be stuck with me after he rejects me? Except I'm not sure I'll even have a home anymore after this.

Ranger swings his legs over the side of the bed and stands up. "I'm going to get some air, and I'll be back in a few minutes, okay?"

I force a smile. "Sure. Anything you need."

My heart is in my throat as I watch him walk out of the motel room, the door clicking shut quietly behind him.

"Well, I'm an absolute idiot," I mutter, and Doc brays, no doubt in agreement. "Hey, excuse you, but I didn't see you giving me much advice here." I look over at PP, resting at the foot of the bed. "And *you*. It's your fault I'm in this mess to begin with. You weren't supposed to let me kiss him."

She doesn't seem the least bit repentant about her role in all this. Typical.

27

RANGER

I haven't smoked a cigarette in a year, but I desperately need one now. Thank fuck there's a gas station two blocks down that sells them. The cashier doesn't even blink when I walk in with Benny, who's wearing his service dog harness like always.

"Beautiful dog," he comments when I'm at the counter. He's a cute kid, not a day older than eighteen, if I had to guess.

"Thank you"—I peer at his name tag—"Tim. He is. One pack of Lucky's, please."

Tim grabs the cigarettes and rings them up. "If you don't mind me asking, why do you have a service dog?"

I eye him for a second. He meets my gaze with a steady calmness, showing genuine interest. "I have PTSD, and he's trained to help with that."

This may be the first time I've ever spoken those words to anyone else, and they're much easier than I expected.

Tim's eyes light up. "Really? That's so cool. Well, not that you have PTSD, but that your dog can help with that." Then his face grows serious. "I should tell my brother about this."

I frown as I hand him cash. "He's a vet?"

"Yes. He came back from Afghanistan a few months ago. Lost his right leg due to an IED. He's been...struggling. I'm worried about him."

My face softens. "You should be. It's a tough adjustment for him." I've been lucky myself to walk away unharmed—physically at least—but I've seen plenty of men who lost limbs.

"Do you think he'd be able to get a dog?"

"Do you have a pen and paper for me?"

Tim hands me a pen and, after some rumbling in a drawer, a note block that was white once upon a time. I write down the name and website of Pups for Patriots, then add Julian's number. "I can't answer that, but this is the charity that helped me get a dog. Contact them or have your parents do it and ask about his chances of getting approved for one. Once he is, contact this guy. His name is Julian, and he trains these dogs. He trained Benny as well." I nod at Benny, who's been patiently sitting right beside me, like the good boy he is.

"Thank you." Tim carefully rips the paper off the note block, then folds it and puts it in his pocket. "I'll give them a call. I want him to become better, you know?"

"He'll never be the same," I warn him. "You can't go through something like that without it changing you."

"I understand that. I just want him to be happy again, to feel like he has a reason to live."

When I got Benny, that's how I felt about him. Like he'd given me a reason to get out of bed, to keep the house at least somewhat tidy because he lived there too. I never expected myself to grow as attached to him as I have.

"You're a good brother," I tell Tim, then walk out.

"Thank you for your service!" Tim calls after me.

I never know what to say when people tell me that. "You're welcome" sounds so stupid and cliché. "My pleasure" is woefully inadequate, and so are any variations on "anytime." So I usually grunt, hoping that people will accept that as an acceptable response.

As soon as I'm away from the gas station, I light my cigarette, inhaling deeply. Now, to prevent a lecture: I normally don't smoke. Not really, but in certain situations, smoking a cigarette has proven to be a stress relief. Like after an operation we did. Never before. But I'd share a pack with my guys afterward, and that would be that. It became a ritual that we clung to in a life where so much was uncertain.

Always Lucky's. It was our brand, mine and Lucky's. We smoked our first one as teenagers, choking on it. Thank fuck neither of us is sensitive to addictions. But the preference for that brand stayed, and it was how my brother got his nickname.

All this to say is that I'm not gonna smoke the whole damn pack; I just need a goddamn cigarette because I don't know what to do with myself after what Julian said.

I guess Lucky was right. Julian really does like me. I have no fucking clue why because even though I can see I've made progress, I'm still a grumpy, depressed guy without a real job or decent prospects in life. Luckily, I saved up enough money to buy my house in cash, and I live quite frugally, but at some point, I'll need to get a job, and I have no idea what I could do without my PTSD fucking it up.

Not that Julian would need me to be the breadwinner. He's built an excellent life for himself, and even though he's facing a big setback, he'll get back up. He's too determined, too stubborn not to. No, he doesn't need me financially...and in fact, I don't even think he cares about money. He's never brought it up.

He likes you for you. The voice in my head sounds like the voice-over of a Hallmark movie, all warm and understanding. The voice of reason, except that to me, that cliché doesn't sound reasonable at all. He likes me for me? What the fuck? My body, okay. I could understand that. But me as a person?

Ten years ago, sure. I was witty, strong, had a career. I'm not saying I was carefree because I don't think I've ever been. That's not how I'm wired. But I didn't have this load on my shoulders that has been crushing me.

Although lately, the dark clouds over my head seem more gray than black, the edges more silver lined each day. All because of Julian. He's brought happiness and light into my life, driving away the painful memories and distressing thoughts. If I let him, he'd change me into a happy little beam of sunshine just like him.

If I let him. If I let him into my life, into my heart. If I dare to take this crazy step, this big jump into the unknown and start something real with him. If I stop being afraid and have the courage to admit what we both know: what we have between us was never casual. How could it be, with me being who I am and he so caring and invested? The guy loves animals so much that we turned our motel room into a nativity scene with only a baby missing. And the virgin Mary, but maybe my gay virginity counts?

I snort at my own joke, even though it was godawful. God, how pathetic. I've reached that stage now, where you laugh at your own jokes while everyone else thinks they suck. Whatever. I'll take my joy where I can find it.

Like with Julian. He makes me happy. He makes me want to be a better man. He chases away the darkness. No matter what happens, no matter how our relationship ends, right now, that's enough. And I not only deserve that; I want to embrace it.

I don't know why he wants me, but maybe I don't need to know. Maybe it's enough to trust he's telling the truth and let this take its course. Because even if we break up at some point, which I absolutely count on, I'll still be a better person for having been allowed to spend this time with him.

My mind made up, I make my way back to the motel room.

28

JULIAN

There's a donkey on the bed.

It's not my fault that Doc felt bad for me after Ranger left to get some air. PP really doesn't seem that amused by the situation, but I feel a bit better lying on the bed with Doc's head on my chest, stroking the soft fur between his eyes.

Ranger's been gone so long I'm half convinced he got in his truck and just kept heading north, leaving my needy butt in his rearview mirror. I've been too afraid to get up and check. I wouldn't blame him. I told him I was fine with casual and then went and started talking about feelings a few weeks later. It's bad hookup etiquette; everyone knows that.

The door to the room eases open, and I hear a sigh before he's even all the way back in the room.

"So, this is a thing, huh?" he asks, sounding halfway between amused and resigned.

"Doc, get down." I sign at him, but he just pushes his head harder against my chest, pretending like he doesn't know what I'm telling him to do. "Sorry, I wasn't sure if you were coming back."

He arches an eyebrow at me. "And if I wasn't, you were going to spoon with a donkey the rest of the night?"

I shrug. "It seemed like a solid enough plan."

Ranger chuckles as I finally manage to sit up and coax Doc off the bed with a minimal amount of annoyed braying and dirty looks.

"What did you mean, this is a thing?" I ask because that's easier than asking what sent him fleeing from the room.

He climbs onto the bed. Benny hops up as well and makes himself comfortable at the foot of the bed next to PP. The smell of cigarette smoke clinging to Ranger's clothes wafts around me as he kicks off his shoes and lets them drop one at a time with a thud next to the bed.

"I meant that I shouldn't be surprised that my boyfriend would let a donkey in the bed as soon as I step outside." He smirks. My heart does its level best to leap out of my chest.

"Boyfriend?" I can't stop the smile from spreading across my face.

"That's what you were saying before I left, wasn't it? Or am I getting this all wrong? Are we supposed to have a few proper dates before slapping on the boyfriend label? Because I'd argue that we've already had a few. We just didn't call them dates at the time. Plus, we're spending the weekend in a motel together, which feels like it should count as one or two."

"Not sure I'd bring Doc on a date if given the choice," I reason, still smiling like a fool as I scoot closer to Ranger until our chests are pressed together and our legs are intertwined.

"You let him in the bed. I'm not sure where you draw the

line," he teases, cupping my jaw with his hand and rubbing his thumb along my cheek. I tilt my head into his touch, closing my eyes and savoring the moment.

"You mean it?" I ask after a few seconds.

"About Doc being in the bed?"

"No." I snort, gathering the fabric of his T-shirt in my fists and resting my forehead against his. "You want to be my boyfriend?"

"I mean it," he answers without hesitation. "I like you too, J. Honestly, I don't get what you see in me, but...I'm not ready to cut this off. I want to see what happens."

It's not exactly a declaration of undying love, but I'm one hundred percent okay with that right now.

I tug on the front of his shirt and smash my mouth against his, happiness bubbling up inside me, knowing that Ranger likes me. Okay, I know that's a bit juvenile, but *Ranger likes me back!!!!*

Our lips move together in a slow, sweet kiss that picks up steam as it goes on. He slips his tongue into my mouth and strokes it against mine, hot and heavy. I can taste the cigarette on his tongue as well, but it's not enough to stop kissing him.

Unfortunately, a sharp, unwelcome pain ruins the moment. Even without the self-satisfied braying, I would've been able to guess who was to blame.

"Ow! Mother of Bacon Bits," I squeal, throwing myself half on top of Ranger to escape getting another bite on my ass from Doc.

"That hurt, you know. I wanted our *second* kiss stopped, not this one."

"He was supposed to stop our second kiss?" Ranger asks.

"PP was. I'm glad she didn't, but at the time it seemed

like a bad idea to kiss you, so I told her to save me from myself."

Doc butts my elbow with his nose, then tugs at my T-shirt with his teeth again. Meanwhile, the girls decide this is a great time to flap around inside their makeshift cage.

I sigh. Talk about getting cockblocked.

"Maybe we should wait until things are a little less *Wild Kingdom*," Ranger suggests.

"I loved that show as a kid," I muse, eyeing Doc and considering the options. The bathroom could work, but it's a little small, and frankly, motel bathrooms skeeve me out. I catch sight of the keys to my truck resting on the nightstand, and I grin.

"Let's go have sex in the truck."

"What if someone sees us?" His husky purr is more than enough to tell me he isn't opposed to the idea.

"Then I guess it'll be their lucky day." I slide off the bed and open the side zipper on my duffle bag, grabbing a condom and the bottle of lube I stashed in there. Clothes, family heirlooms, and safe sex supplies, the essentials every "go-bag" needs.

I hold up the supplies, waving the condom at Ranger. "Come on, it'll be fun."

He scrambles off the bed and follows me out to my truck.

With the bench seat in front, trucks are so much more convenient for vehicular sex than cars could ever hope to be. I said what I said.

We both climb in, and I toss the supplies onto the dash for safekeeping, then crawl onto Ranger's lap. Straddling his thighs and wrapping my arms around his neck, I go in for another kiss.

He was right. This is much better without the four-legged audience. His hands find their way onto my ass, grabbing and kneading it through my jeans, while our tongues tangle as we kiss and grind against each other. The hard bulge of his cock presses against mine through our pants. Our heavy breaths fog up the windows in no time, creating the illusion of privacy, even out in the parking lot.

"I know you don't see it, but you really stepped up and saved the day today," I murmur against his lips between kisses, dragging my fingers through his hair.

Ranger huffs. I'm not sure if it's meant to be a scoff or a laugh. Either way, it's obvious he doesn't believe my praise. That's okay. I'm happy to keep talking until he believes me.

I kiss my way along his jaw, circling my hips against his, the steel outline of his cock rubbing against mine and making my body ache. I want him to fill me, stretch me, fuck me until I can't walk right tomorrow.

"You were level-headed and in charge. It was so hot." I nip at the hard edge of his jaw. "You knew exactly what needed to happen, and you got it done." I kiss my way down his throat, then suck on his Adam's apple. "You're capable and strong and so sexy I can hardly think straight sometimes."

Ranger moans, digging his fingers harder into my ass. "You're too sweet to me." His voice is a deep, raspy rumble.

"Too bad. Learn to live with it." I grab the hem of his shirt and yank it up over his head.

"I don't deserve you." He takes my shirt off and tosses it aside as well, then pulls me in for another kiss.

"Life's too short for that kind of thinking, baby. You deserve everything you want."

"I want to fuck you." He tugs my bottom lip between his

teeth, then gives a soothing lick, thrusting up against me at the same time.

"So glad we're on the same page because I'm about to die if you don't get inside me soon."

We kiss harder, deeper, hungrier as we fumble with the button on each other's jeans.

29

RANGER

It's chaotic and uncoordinated, elbows and knees getting in the way as we bump into each other, but we manage to undress, sharing sloppy, eager kisses in between. I'm grateful for the limited visibility outside and the tinted windows of Julian's truck. If not for that, we might've had an audience for what we're about to do.

I'm about to fuck him. Part of me protests at our first time together being in a truck, and yet it feels strangely appropriate. Nothing about our relationship has been normal.

The sensation of his naked skin against mine makes me even harder, which I didn't think was possible. "I want you so bad," I whisper, but it comes out more like a growl.

"Ditto." Julian's voice is as hoarse as mine.

I take his mouth again, unable to resist the temptation of his swollen, red lips. I want to drown myself in his taste, his smell, the featherlight touch of his fingers, the way he holds on to my shoulders as he rubs his body against mine like a horny stallion. So. Fucking. Hot.

He's on my lap again, our cocks pressing against each

other, trapped between our bodies. "What do I do?" Of course I know the mechanics, but doing this in a car is a little different, and I don't want to hurt him.

"Under other circumstances..."

He nips at my bottom lip.

"I would love for you to prep me..."

His lips trail to my ear, and his teeth scrape my earlobe, sending shivers down my spine.

"But in this case..."

He sucks hard on that supersensitive spot behind my ear, and I'm pretty sure I'll have a mark to show for it later. Why is that thought so thrilling?

"I'll gladly do it myself so we can get this show on the road."

I eye the dashboard off the truck. "Metaphorically speaking, I hope."

He leans back and looks at me with a puzzled frown. "Huh?"

"I just wanted to make clear that the 'on the road' part wasn't literally because driving while fucking you seems a tad ambitious for my first time. We can always do that later on when I'm more proficient at the whole getting naked and getting it on."

It takes him a second, but then he bursts out laughing, his body shaking with the force of it. I grin, stupidly happy I made him laugh.

"Holy bananas, that was funny," Julian says when he's finally calmed down. Then he cups my cheeks, his eyes warm, and presses a tender kiss on my lips. "Thank you for making me laugh today. I needed that."

He kisses me again, slower this time, and we settle into a different rhythm, one less frantic yet so much more intense. Julian sits astride my lap, his legs folded backward in what has to be uncomfortable, but he's not complaining.

The faint light spilling in from outside shimmers over Julian's smooth skin, making him glow. "You're so beautiful," I whisper against his lips. "So goddamn breathtaking."

"So are you."

No more words are needed as his tongue meets mine again, luring me deeper into his mouth until I can't think of anything else but him. He grabbles on the dashboard for the things he brought, then proves just how talented he is at multitasking as he keeps kissing me while he preps himself, devouring my mouth until the kiss consumes me, setting me on fire in a way I never experienced before.

He's everywhere—around me, in me, over me, under me. His mouth tastes like the most expensive whiskey, the flavor bold on my tongue. Goose bumps pebble on my skin, where he scratches and strokes, claws and caresses. And his scent, his tantalizing scent, salty and sweet with a hint of tangy sharpness. I breathe in deeply, and something settles deep inside me. He smells like sunshine and happiness, like safety. Like home.

He finally breaks off the kiss, tears open the condom, and rolls it onto my cock. I wait, my heart galloping, as he puts some more lube on it.

"Let me do this part," Julian says, and I nod.

He shifts until he's found a good position, and I sink as low on the bench as I can. Then he holds my dick with one hand and lowers himself, and all I can do is put my hands lightly on his slender hips and watch, mesmerized. He bites his bottom lip, his brows furrowed in concentration.

His hole presses against me, and I gasp as he lets me in. Tight, slick heat envelops my cock as Julian works himself down my length, inch by inch. Every slide of his hips brings me deeper inside him, increasing that unbelievable grip on my cock. I'm already far closer to my release than I want.

Finally, I'm buried to the hilt, and he holds still, his hands on my shoulders. Our eyes lock as he rises and sinks back down, and my fingers dig into his hips to help him. He does it again and again, and I swear, I have to fight for control and not batter into him like a rutting bull.

I don't have words for how I feel, my body overloaded with sensations. Bliss, pure, explosive bliss radiates from my cock into my balls, my lower belly, my whole body. Every nerve is alive, more alive than I've ever felt in my life.

Julian throws back his head, and with closed eyes, he rides me. He's breathtaking. I've traveled all over the world and witnessed some pretty spectacular views, but I can't think of anything more beautiful than Julian taking his pleasure from my body. The faint red glow from outside makes him otherworldly, like a mythical creature, and oh my fucking god, I'm buried deep inside him, and I'm getting all misty-eyed and poetic, fucking sap that I am.

I stop trying to find words for what's happening and, instead, surrender to the need thundering through my veins. I meet him halfway now, responding to the siren's call that's as old as time. Even though I've never done this before, my body knows what to do. We fit together, move together, completely in sync, as if we've danced to the same song for years.

No more kisses now, our breaths coming too fast to manage that. He moans, and I grunt; he makes this high whimpering, and I respond with a low growl as he once again sinks down, taking me in all the way. I want to stay inside him. I want him to ride me forever. I want…

I want so much more than I should, so much more than

is smart, but I can't help it. I want. I want him, whichever way I can get him.

His movements become fast and furious, and I lose all ability to think. His hips roll and undulate. I take his cock in my hand, his pulse beating against my skin, and I circle his crown in a firm grip.

"Like that... Oh, shit. *Shit!* Yes, exactly like that."

The fact that I made Julian swear says it all. I grit my teeth, fighting back the wave building inside me. "I can't hold out much longer..."

My chest aches, and I don't know if it's from how fast my heart is beating or from my panting breaths or from this feeling inside me that's too big for words. My hips rock as I thrust upward to meet him, fast snaps, slapping our flesh together.

"Ranger..." he says on a breathy exhale. "Please..."

My hand squeezes him tighter, desperate to bring him pleasure first, and then he explodes. His body shakes uncontrollably as his cock spurts out its load into my hand. He tightens around my cock, and it all but kills me to hold back. But I don't want to miss it. I don't want to be so overwhelmed that I miss out on his pleasure.

I pump his cock, my grip lessening in strength, until he's done. Only then do I let go, a growl coming out from the back of my throat as my hips move, thrusting inside him with all my strength. His cries mingle with my low, deep groans as the wave reaches its crescendo, rolling over me, and pleasure explodes in my body everywhere—my cock, my balls, my belly, the very tip of my toes, and in my heart.

Julian holds on to me, pressing his body against mine, his hands wrapped around my neck now, and I bury my face in his hair. When my body finally stops shivering and shuddering, it aches from the violence of my orgasm, and I'm so exhausted I could fall asleep right then and there.

"That was..." I say.

"Yeah."

"I don't have words."

"Words are hard," Julian agrees, and I smile in his hair, reveling in the sensation of his body still linked to mine.

"I guess we're gonna have to move sometime soon?"

"Considering I've about lost feeling in my toes from being so cramped, that'd be good." He releases me, and I do the same as he leans back. "But totally worth it."

His sweet smile makes my heart dance. "Yeah?"

"I'd rate ten out of ten, would do it again."

I'm still smiling when we rush back into our room, our half-dressed state getting some amused looks from a few people walking in the parking lot. I don't care. And neither do I care that all throughout our shower, Doc is making his displeasure about the lack of attention for him known. That donkey will not cockblock me again.

30

JULIAN

My heart is in my throat the entire drive back to my place. Ranger reaches over from the passenger seat of my truck and squeezes my knee. It's been a week since I evacuated, and we were just given the all clear this morning to go back to my farm.

The fire ended up missing Ranger's house completely, his county being allowed back in their homes after the first couple of days, which was convenient because I'm not sure how long I was actually going to get away with keeping Doc and my chickens in a motel room.

We've spent the past five days at Ranger's place, letting Doc and the chickens roam on his land while the two of us kept busy building a barn. I have no idea if he actually needed a barn built or if it was his way of keeping my mind off worrying about my house and my horses. Either way, it worked, and he got a barn out of the deal. If there are better distractions than sex and manual labor, I haven't found them yet.

"Whatever we find, it's going to be okay," he promises

me, and all I can do is nod, unable to trust my own voice right now.

PP whines from the backseat, straining against her seat belt, no doubt wanting to put her head on my shoulder to comfort me. I take a few deep breaths, reminding myself that I'm alive, as many of my babies as I could manage are alive, and the rest was out of my hands. Ranger's right. Everything will be okay, one way or another.

That light optimism lasts me until I pull into my driveway and see the pile of ashes that used to be my house. I put the truck into Park, a sob breaking free from my throat at the sight in front of me. My fields are razed to the ground, and every structure that once stood is now nothing more than smoking cinders.

I throw open the door and stumble out of the truck, the sound of PP's frantic bark little more than background noise as my blood rushes in my ears.

Everything is gone. Every last thing I owned, save for the few items now at Ranger's, has been turned to charcoal. The house I scraped and saved to buy? Gone. The fence I built and rebuilt by hand? Gone. It's all gone.

As soon as Ranger's arms wrap around me, I sink into him, pressing my face against his shoulder and soaking his shirt with my tears. My body shakes with the force of my sobs, his strong embrace the only thing keeping me in one piece.

I'm not sure how long I stand there, getting snot and tears all over my boyfriend, but eventually I calm down enough to register the fact that PP's bark has changed. It's no longer the frustrated whine she makes when she's being prevented from doing something she wants—in this case comforting me. It's her excited yap. It's rare to hear in her old age. Rare enough that I manage to wipe my eyes with the back of my hand and pull away from Ranger to see what she's getting worked up about.

At first, it seems like she's just being strange. I look around and don't see anything other than the devastation that met us when we drove up. PP runs a few yards away from us, then comes bounding back, still yipping. I sniffle and use my own T-shirt to dry my face, Ranger's hand now resting on the back of my neck as he waits stoically beside me.

"What is it, girl? What do you see?" I crouch, sling my arm around her, and follow her line of sight. A flash of purple bobs in the farthest field. My heart jumps, a flicker of hope taking root inside my chest.

"Is that…?" I'm afraid to say it out loud in case I'm wrong, but as the spec of color surges closer and closer, a laugh bubbles from my throat, raw from my tears. "It's Butler."

I should've known that stubborn goat would be just fine. The cloud that settled over me lifts just as quickly. A house can be replaced, even all the things inside the house can be bought again. If even one of my animals is okay, I'll take that trade in a heartbeat.

I break into a jog toward Butler. He's still far enough away that I'm not going to run all the way to him, but I'm too excited to stand and wait. As I get closer, I realize he's not alone. It was easy to spot him because of the tattered pool noodles still on his horns, but the smaller black goat beside him comes as a surprise.

In spite of his years of animosity, Butler seems as thrilled to see me as I am to see him, and he trots through the field faster and faster until he reaches me. I want to drop to my knees and throw my arms around him, but I doubt he's grown *that* fond of me in the span of the last week, so I settle for patting his head.

New tears flow down my cheeks, relieved ones this time. "I'm so happy to see you." I sniffle and laugh at the same time. "And who's your friend?"

I turn to the new goat, which is sticking close to my boy, and slowly reach out my arm. He bleats and gently butts against my hand. He's friendlier than Butler, that's for sure. "Don't worry, buddy. We'll find your family," I assure him. Butler doesn't seem on board with that plan, though, getting between us and putting his back to me as he nuzzles his new friend.

Well, okay then. I guess once I find his family, I can see if they're open to a visitation schedule or something because I don't think my boy here is going to let him go.

I scan the charred tree line, my hope renewed and my optimism possibly a little too high now. To my amazement and relief, new movement catches my eye, and seconds later, Talon emerges from the trees, followed by Dino, and one by one, all five of my babies appear.

It feels like every single Christmas and birthday all rolled into one, and joy bursts through me like fireworks as my horses gallop toward me, whinnying and snorting. They're all a bit sooty, their manes tangled, and the acrid smell of smoke is clinging to them. They'll need baths and a thorough check by their vet, but they're all alive. Each and every one of them is okay.

I wrap my arms around Bella's neck and hug her tightly while Butler's new friend nibbles on my shirt. Daisy brings up the rear while Raleigh noses at my pocket in the hope of finding an apple no doubt. Lucky for him, I *did* bring apples in case I found them. I pull the baggie out and pass out apple slices to each of my babies, sniffling the whole time.

I probably look like a horse whisperer, walking back

toward Ranger with five horses and two goats all following me closely.

"Is this everybody?" Ranger asks.

"Every last one." I smile through the happy tears that won't stop flowing. "It'll be tight, but all five horses should squeeze into the trailer, and the goats can ride in the dog kennel in the bed of the truck.

"Um, is it just me, or have you gained a goat?" He frowns at Buddy, the name I am officially giving to Butler's new friend, and scratches his head.

"It looks that way."

The goats are exhausted and dehydrated enough that they don't fight me putting them into the dog cage. Once everyone is loaded up, I climb back into the truck and sink into the seat with a relieved sigh.

"Good thing we got that barn built, huh?" Ranger jokes.

"Fiddlesticks, I should've asked if you're even okay with all of us coming back to your place." If he says no, I have no clue where to go. I could try to find a boarding facility for the horses until I work out my housing situation, but it'll be difficult to find a place willing to take so many on such short notice, not to mention *pricey*.

"Hey." He threads his fingers through mine. "Of course they can come to my place. You have all the time you need. I'm glad they're all okay."

"Me too." I bring his hand to my lips and press a quick kiss to the back of it. "And thank you for giving us a place to stay while I figure everything out. I don't know what I'd do otherwise."

"Of course. What are boyfriends for?" He gives me a lopsided grin, leaning in to kiss me.

"Blow jobs mostly. But help with housing crises is always a bonus."

31

RANGER

Living with Julian is surprisingly easy. I thought I'd need time to get used to him, especially since he brought his whole menagerie with him, but it's been a smooth transition.

I can't believe all his animals survived the fire when so many didn't. I don't know if it's because they're smart—though for Butler, that's debatable—or because they would do anything for him. Maybe both.

Fact is that I've never built a fence faster in my life, and it now holds five horses and a donkey. When I purchased this house, I never thought I'd use the acreage that came with it. I'd bought it mostly to ensure my privacy and because the land came with water rights. At the time, I wasn't sure what I was gonna do with my life, but somewhere in the back of my mind was the thought that no matter what I'd do, access to water would come in handy, and here we are.

Having the animals here means sticking to a routine, which I'm already used to, thanks to Julian being here for three weeks. I get up when he does, and together, we check on the animals, fill their water troughs, and feed them.

I love that quiet time in the morning with him, when he hasn't done his hair yet, and it's sticking up in every direction. When he uses funny voices to talk to all the animals, and I swear they understand every word he says. When he still has those heavy-lidded eyes and that dopey, sleepy smile. When he's snuggly and wants to cuddle on the couch with our first cup of coffee as soon as we're back inside. He's adorable. I never thought I'd say that about a man and mean it in the very best way imaginable.

After coffee, we shower. Usually together, another new routine I've come to appreciate. He's often handsy in the shower, and I love how confident he is in his touch.

And then I work. Gone are the days where I'd look at the clock and wonder how I had spent a whole day on the couch and not notice. There's too much to do, and it's given me a sense of purpose that had been missing.

I've built extra shelves in my bedroom so Julian has a place to put his clothes. He didn't bring much, but we've bought new shirts and pants, and the shelves are slowly filling. Julian tackled cleaning the kitchen, which, I'm embarrassed to admit, was way past due. He waved off my mumbled apologies for the sorry state it was in, repeating that he understood until I stopped apologizing, accepting he really didn't care.

I've fixed the potholes in the driveway, checked the roof for possible leaks, cut down a dead tree, and my next project is the master bathroom, which desperately needs an update. The tiles are baby blue and most likely dating back to the eighties. 'Nuff said.

"You're very handy," Julian muses. He's sitting on one of the rocking chairs on the porch while I stand on a ladder, installing a diversion from the gutter into a rain barrel system I bought. Those water rights are going to pay off big-time, and with this many animals, we use a lot of water each day. It doesn't rain that often, but when it does, I want to catch every drop.

"I like working with my hands." I critically inspect the tightness of the screws. Yes, that should do the job.

"You're good at it."

I shrug, then carefully climb down the ladder. "Learned a lot from my dad when I was young and then in the Army. I've always had a practical, problem-solving mind, and I'm good at picking up technical skills, stuff you can do with your hands."

"Maybe you can do that for the long term."

We've talked about the future. Hesitantly, neither of us willing to risk too much by going too fast, but I told him I have about a year more of savings before I need to get more serious about earning an income.

"Like being a handyman?"

"Sure. Or a contractor for smaller things. I'm sure that if you put your mind to it, you could learn to do even more."

I wipe my brow off with a bandana and then lower myself in the other rocking chair. "That's not a bad idea, actually. I joined the Army straight out of high school. It's not like I have a broad set of skills that's easily transferable to civilian life."

"Ranger..."

He sounds pained, and I frown. "What?"

"You're so dismissive of your skills, of your talents and expertise."

I look at my hands, which are rough and blistered from my hard work in the last few weeks. "My talent is being a soldier. It's killing the enemy and hopefully preventing myself and my team from getting killed."

"Is that how you regard your brother?"

I've told him about Lucky and his men, and he's excited to meet them. We actually have a tentative plan to go sailing next Saturday, god help me. But why is Julian bringing up Lucky?

"No, of course not. First of all, he was a Marine, which a lot more people hold in higher esteem. Rangers aren't as well known. And second, he's supersmart. He's a parole officer, but he could've easily become an FBI agent or something. He did go to college, has the degree and all, like you, and he can read people like a book."

Julian is quiet for a long time, his face serious and pensive. "I did a little research into the Rangers," he finally says.

"You did?"

"I'd heard of them, but I wasn't sure what they did exactly. The more I read, the more impressed I was."

As always, I'm deeply uncomfortable with praise like that. I don't know why it's so hard for me to accept it, but I can't. "Thank you?"

"I looked at the numbers. There are way more Marines than there are Rangers."

"Yes."

"You can join the Marines straight out of high school, but going to Ranger School is awarded to the best soldiers to start with, and only the best of those are selected to actually join the Ranger regiment. You were selected for that elite unit."

Wow, he's really done his research. "Yes. I was part of the 75th regiment, second battalion out of Fort Lewis, Washington."

"The courses to get there are insanely difficult."

I think back on Ranger School when I became familiar

with levels of exhaustion I'd never known before. "Yeah. It's no walk in the park."

He gets up from his chair, then walks over to me and kneels between my legs, putting his hands on my knees. "I don't know what happened to you that you've come to look down on yourself when you were selected for one of the most elite troops our country has. No offense to your brother, but your odds to get in were way, way smaller than his."

Huh. He's right. I knew that, rationally, but I've always looked up to Lucky, even though he's my younger brother. He just seemed so put together, even after he left the Marines. So many men I knew struggled with the transition to civilian life, but his was seamless. He made a plan, and he followed it, rolling from one career into the other without problems. Unlike me.

He left when he was ready. He left of his own accord, on his own timing. You didn't. You were honorably discharged because you had to be, because you were no longer fit to serve.

I knew that. Of course I did. But it's never hit me like this, and suddenly, it all makes sense. "I compare myself to him," I say, my voice raw and hoarse. "He made it look so easy when he got out, and I struggled so much. It made me feel like I was less than him. Less capable, less skilled. Just...less."

Julian's eyes are full of compassion. "I figured. Did he ever say something to that effect? Because if he did, he and I need to have a word."

The idea of Julian confronting my badass Marine brother is incredibly sweet, and my heart fills with gratitude for the day this man walked into my life. "No, that's all me. Rationally, I know that having PTSD doesn't mean you're weak, but..."

"It's hard not to feel that way deep inside," Julian finishes my sentence, and I nod.

"I guess I still judged myself for it, for needing time to recover. For not being as perfect as Lucky."

Julian harrumphs. "I sincerely doubt your brother is perfect. When we go sailing, let's ask his boyfriends to list all his bad habits and annoying quirks. I'm sure he has a few."

That idea is wonderfully appealing, and I smile. "He's pretty full of himself at times. When he's convinced he's right, he'll steamroll right over your objections. And he snores like a fucking freight train."

Julian throws up his hands. "See? Far from perfect."

I let out a deep sigh, and with it, some more of the weight I've been carrying around for far too long. "My journey may be a longer one than I want...a longer one than I had counted on and maybe than I have the patience for."

Julian takes my hands and kisses them one by one. "There's no timeline for this. And we both know some of it may never heal...and that's okay too. As long as you have hope."

"Yeah," I say hoarsely. "I've got hope."

32

JULIAN

"Is this right on him?" Ranger asks, worrying at the lifejacket Benny has on, double-checking each of the straps.

I already checked it, but I give it another look to ease his worries. I slip my fingers under to check that it's tight enough without rubbing against his skin anywhere and pull on each strap to make sure they're firmly in place. "It feels perfect. Remember, it's only a precaution. He's a good swimmer too."

Ranger lets out a long breath. "Right, sorry. I just don't want anything bad to happen to him. I don't want to let him down."

My heart squeezes, and I press a kiss against his stubbled cheek. He still hasn't told me what had happened before he was discharged, but it's obvious that even with as much progress as he's made since we met, he still blames himself for whatever it was. Maybe he always will on some level.

"You're taking great care of him, and I think he's taking good care of you too."

He nods. "You both are."

Benny wags his tail, gazing longingly at the water he's able to see from our place in the parking lot. A lesser-trained Golden would bolt for the ocean and splash right in, but he knows his job is to stay with Ranger, and he'll do it, even when part of his instincts are telling him to do something else. That's the beauty of the strength of the pack bond. His pack comes first. It's an admirable trait in dogs.

I stand back up, and Ranger does the same. I have to say, he looks awfully cute dressed in his sailing clothes—a light T-shirt and a pair of slightly tattered cargo shorts, a pair of Aviators giving him an even more badass vibe than he usually has.

I reach back into the front seat of the truck to grab the bottle of sunscreen that's lying there, squirting a generous amount into the palm of my hands and coating my skin. When I end up with extra, I beckon Ranger forward and use it to cover his face.

"There. We have to protect that handsome face."

He snorts and grins, looping an arm around my middle and pulling me in to plant a kiss against my neck. After the fire, I was worried things were moving too fast, that having to crash with him for a little while might mess up our relationship or scare him off, but if anything, it feels like it's brought us closer together. The L-word has been dancing in the back of my mind, but I'm afraid it's still too soon for him, so I'm keeping a lid on that for now.

"I'm excited for you to meet my brother and his partners today," he says, grabbing my hand once I put the sunblock away. We head toward the dock, Benny following us.

"Me too. It's the perfect first official date for us," I tease. Because of everything that's been going on, we still haven't gotten around to our first "real" date. I don't mind so much, but it's become a fun thing between Ranger and me.

"It's not our first official date. That's going to be romantic and fantastic and just the two of us," he insists.

"One day." I sigh dramatically, and he groans at me. Having a boyfriend to tease is so much fun.

As we draw close to the docks, I spot three men already waiting for us, and a bout of nerves flutters in my stomach. What if Lucky doesn't like me? He and Ranger are so close if I don't get his approval, this relationship is basically over.

Great, way to freak yourself out, Julian.

"Are you okay?" Ranger asks, squeezing my hand.

"Yup, I am a tasty peach cobbler topped with ice cream."

"What?" He chuckles.

"Peachy." I shoot him a crooked smile.

It's easy to tell which one is Lucky. Not just because Ranger drops my hand to hug his brother as soon as we reach them, but because the man is *clearly* a former marine —muscular, short hair, a resting badass face that's washed away as he smiles at his brother.

"You're looking good," he murmurs, patting Ranger on the back before they part.

"I'm feeling good," Ranger says, grabbing my hand again. "Better than I've felt in a long time. And it's all thanks to these two."

"It's all thanks to yourself. Benny and I are just here to help when you need it," I correct because he shouldn't minimize the work he's been putting in. If he hadn't wanted to get better, then a hundred therapy dogs and blow jobs wouldn't have made any bit of difference. "I'm Julian." I hold out my hand to Lucky.

"I've heard a lot about you. It's great to finally meet you."

I draw up short for a fraction of a second as I hold my

hand out to the next man. I've definitely seen him in porn, and I'm not sure if that's a polite thing to mention or not. "Heart," he introduces himself. "And yes, I used to be with the Ballsy Boys. It's okay. I'm not ashamed of it."

"Sorry, I really need to work on my indoor face." I shake his hand. "I wonder if Dear Abby has ever covered that one—etiquette when meeting a former pornstar."

They all laugh. "She definitely should," Heart agrees.

The third man is all kinds of adorable with messy, curly hair and a general nerdy vibe. He steps forward and nearly trips over his own feet. This seems to be a common occurrence because Heart catches him without flinching, clearly ready for it. He's also the only of the three wearing a lifejacket, and we're not even on the boat yet.

"Mason." He gives me a shy smile.

"Nice to meet all of you."

Benny sidles up and sniffs at each of them. "We're not supposed to pet him, right?" Mason checks.

"You can," Ranger answers. "Generally no with a service dog, but since Benny is technically *always* on duty, and you're not a stranger, I'm okay with it."

Mason grins, crouching and scratching Benny's favorite spot behind his ears.

I've never been on a sailboat—or any kind of boat for that matter—and it turns out they're not exactly easy to get onto.

"Isn't there supposed to be some kind of ramp?" I wobble with one foot on the dock, the other on the side of the boat. Ranger and Benny went ahead of me; both of them got on without any trouble. I may be overthinking it.

"We're not that fancy around here," Ranger jokes, offering me his hand.

"If you let me fall into the water, I'll have to do terrible things to you." I let go of the docking post, or whatever it's called, and fling myself into the boat.

He catches me with ease, and I let out a relieved breath.

"What kinds of terrible things would you do?" he murmurs.

"Um, I'm not sure. Maybe I could bite you or something?"

"Bite me?" Ranger laughs. "Fuck, you're adorable. You know that, right?"

"Yes, I am well aware of my charms." I grin and kiss him, then find a place to sit next to Heart and Mason while the brothers get this baby moving.

"He really is like a different person since he met you," Heart says quietly. "It's good to see him so happy."

"He's been good for me too." It's not lip service. I don't know what I would've done this past month if it wasn't for Ranger. But more than just the help he's given me, he's made me feel special and happy, and...yup, there's that L-word again creeping its way to the front of my mind.

He's clearly in his element, pulling on ropes and checking things while Lucky unties the cable anchoring us to the dock. He catches me watching and shoots me a wink and a smile that makes my heart flutter.

33

RANGER

We take the boat out of the harbor on the engine, maneuvering slowly to avoid all the other water traffic. It's a gorgeous day, and we're far from the only ones seeking some relief from the scorching temperatures on the water. The danger is that on days like these, the newbies venture out as well—would-be sailors who've steered a boat once or twice and now think they're ready to take her out by themselves. Spoiler alert: they're not.

I handle the engine while Lucky is at the wheel, keeping a close eye on what happens around us and getting out of harm's way. Benny is at my feet or, more accurately, on my feet, and Julian is chatting with Mason and Heart. He looks happy, and my nerves over this outing ease a little bit.

I want him to like Lucky and his men, and I want them to love him as much as I do. Like him, I mean. I frown. It's way too soon to talk about love. Falling in love doesn't happen that fast. Does it? It can't. I've only known him for a few weeks. Okay, months, but still. Love doesn't develop that quickly. Love needs time to grow. I think. Not something I want to dwell on now, not while I need to concentrate…and while Julian is nearby.

We're finally past most of the busy traffic on the water, and the Pacific Ocean stretches out before us, endless and inviting in her majestic beauty. My dad often joked that he'd expected me to join the Navy, not the Army, and he wasn't wrong. I love the water, always have. But Lucky had announced he wanted to join the Marines when he was, like, thirteen, and I chose the Army. Was I comparing myself to him even back then?

With my head leaned back and my eyes closed for a moment, I let the sun warm my face, a gentle breeze offering a welcome relief. It's been way too long since I was out on the water. The last time was with Lucky and his men, over a year ago. Wow. I can't believe I didn't set foot on a boat for that long.

More and more, I realize PTSD is bigger than the triggers and the flashbacks and the anxiety and shit. It's affected my mental energy in a big way, making me want to curl up into a ball and sleep. It's only been lately that I've not only had the physical energy to do something but the mental power as well.

Lucky signals me that it's time to hoist the sails, and the two of us work in the easy companionship we've always had. I turn the bow into the wind while Lucky loosens the main sheet and checks the halyard. Without saying a word, we each run through the mental checklist we've done a thousand times before, and then we hoist the sails.

The wind catches them immediately, and off we go. Mason lets out a little squeal, and Lucky grins. "Hang on, baby," he calls out to him, but Heart's already wrapped his arm around him.

We've picked a perfect day for our sailing trip. The wind

is strong enough to give the boat a good speed but not so forceful it could cause problems for experienced sailors like us. Lucky runs up the two jibs, and I whoop in excitement when they, too, catch the wind. I quickly check on Julian. He's laughing, his face raised toward the sun. We're flying over the water, the wind and sea spray on my face, and my god, it's invigorating.

"Everyone good?" Lucky checks in, and he gets nods from everyone, so we're good to go. They seem to enjoy it as much as we do.

We let her fly for at least twenty minutes until we're far away from everyone else with other boats only in the distance. On my nod, Lucky lets out the sheets until we slow down significantly.

He jerks his head, indicating I should join Julian, and I do, finding a spot next to him. He immediately comes huddling close, a big smile on his face. "I wasn't too sure about the whole sailing thing, but that was awesome. We went so fast!"

"This baby can fly," I say, petting the deck of the boat like a good friend.

"Time for snacks," Lucky announces, and Heart opens the cooler we brought. Julian hands me an ice-cold Coke, winking at me. He knows my preferences well by now.

We chat as we drift on the water, munching on chips and cookies.

"Can we go swimming?" Heart asks.

"Sure," Lucky says. "Just make sure to wear a lifejacket."

We take down the sails completely, and within minutes, Heart and Julian are swimming in the Pacific. Mason is sitting on the lowest step of the stairs, happy to merely have his lower body in the water. Smart man.

"I can't tell you how good it is to see you this happy," Lucky says softly. The two of us have stayed on board and are sitting shoulder to shoulder, watching the others.

"It's been a while."

"He's good for you."

"He is. I still don't know what he sees in me, but I'll take it as long as he's happy with me."

"Ranger..." He's quiet, a frown between his brows.

"What?"

"I don't know if I should bring this up."

"You might as well now that you've already started it."

Lucky lets out a frustrated sigh. "I'm sorry. I should've thought before opening my mouth. Just... Just promise me that if you don't want to talk about this, you'll tell me."

I nod, curious now what's on his heart.

"Why are you always so hard on yourself? You always have been, even as a teen, but it's gotten even worse the last year. I don't understand."

Leave it to Lucky to get right to the heart of the matter, to what I'm only beginning to understand myself. "It's a fair question...one that I don't have all the answers to yet, but that I'm trying to figure out."

I drag a hand through my hair as I gather my thoughts. "I've always compared myself to you. We're close in age, so maybe it's normal, but... I looked up to you. I was the older one, and yet you felt so much more mature to me. You knew you wanted to join the Marines when you were thirteen or so, and you went for that goal single-mindedly. You're so focused and disciplined, and it seemed to come so easy and natural to you..."

"You were *jealous* of me?" Lucky sounds shocked as if he never even considered that possibility.

"In a way, yes. But not negatively jealous. More like...I wanted to be more like you. And when you left the Marines, you did so with your head held high, and you switched to civilian life like it was nothing. I just... I felt like a failure compared to you. I still do."

I hate that my voice breaks near the end. Absolutely goddamn hate it. And I swear that if Lucky so much as touches me in comfort right now, I'll break. Maybe he realizes it because he stays where he is, though the muscles in his arm are twitching.

"I don't know what to say," he says finally. "It's utter and complete bullshit, and deep down, I'm sure you know that, but that's the rational reaction. You can't help how you feel subconsciously."

"No, I can't. And yes, I know it's not true. But I've had some issues convincing my nonrational brain of that."

"Yeah. You should work on that," Lucky jokes lamely.

We sit for a long time, neither of us speaking. Even though it doesn't solve the problem, I still feel better after telling him.

"Did I ever do anything to make you feel like you were less than me?" Lucky then asks, and I shot him a sideways glance. His face is tight, a crease between his brows.

"No. This was all me."

"Are you sure? Because even if it was some stupid joke, some misguided attempt at being funny—which we both know is not my forte—I'll apologize right now. I never, ever meant for you to feel this way."

I lay my hand on his arm. "You didn't. And yes, you don't have a sense of humor, but I love you anyway, bro."

He scoffs, but his mouth pulls up in a faint smile. "Like you're Mr. Hilarious."

"Oh, I'm not. You know who really is funny, though? Julian. He cracks me up."

"You needed someone who made you laugh."

"From your lips to God's ears. Now let's hope I can manage to hang on to him."

"He's in love with you," Lucky says quietly.

"What?" I take my hand off his arm.

"He's head over heels in love with you."

"How the fuck would you know?"

"Because I know what love looks like, you dork. It's how Mason and Heart look at each other and how they both look at me, and I'm pretty sure that every time I'm with my men, I have that same dopey expression, that same gleam in my eyes."

I let that sink in. "He's in love with me?"

"I'm telling you."

If Lucky is right, then why didn't Julian say anything? As soon as I ask myself the question, I know the answer. He was already scared to confess he wanted more than a fling because he thought he was going too fast. No way would he come right out and tell me he loves me.

"Can love grow that quickly?" I ask my brother.

"Love has no time table. For some people, it takes weeks, months, or even years. Others fall in love at first sight. Just listen to your heart."

Here we are, two of the toughest men, with our military background, and we're talking about feelings and shit. Take that, toxic masculinity. This is way better than pretending to be fine any day.

"I haven't told him about Alex yet. He knows there was someone, but no details."

"He deserves to know, but take your time. He loves you

even without knowing all the facts. I doubt that will change."

I nod. He's right. "I need you to tell me how to plan the most romantic date ever. I want next-level cheesy."

"You've come to the right man." Lucky's face splits open in a big grin, and as our men splash carefree in the ocean, he and I plan a date that would make The Bachelor look like amateurs.

34

JULIAN

PP bounds to me as I step inside Ranger's house, completely and utterly drained after meeting with a contractor to discuss the cost of having my house and barn rebuilt. My heart is heavy, but when I lean down to let her lick my cheek, it feels like most of the stress of the day melts away. Dogs really are the best.

"Honey, I'm home," I call out teasingly, patting PP's head, then stroll into the house in search of Ranger. I spent the thirty-minute drive back to his place trying to come up with a solution for my problem. I can't live here with him forever. Well...actually, I happily could, but he hasn't exactly asked. Baby steps. I'm totally fine with baby steps.

I pull my eyebrows together, listening harder when I don't hear a response, not even Benny's nails on the wood floor.

"Ranger?" I call again, making my way back to the bedroom to see if he's taking a nap. The room is empty, but there's a box and a sheet of paper sitting in the center of the bed. A grin spreads slowly over my lips as I step inside and pick up the piece of paper.

. . .

Julian,

Put this on, then come out to the barn.

"Very mysterious," I say to PP. "What do you suppose he's up to?"

She doesn't seem to have any ideas. Either that or he's already sworn her to secrecy. I guess the only way to find out is to do as the note says. I open the box and find a single red rose laid carefully on top of a deep blue suit.

"Fancy. My man has good taste. Although we already knew that, didn't we?" I waggle my eyebrows at PP, who's now lying down at the foot of the bed, clearly uninterested in this fascinating situation.

I strip out of my clothes and get dressed in the suit, which came complete with a soft gray dress shirt and a pair of socks and shoes, but no underwear. Whether it was an oversight or intentional, it looks like I'll be going commando. I bring the rose with me into the kitchen, then snip the steam short and stick the flower behind my ear.

My stomach dances with anticipation as I step outside. The sun is just starting to set, casting a dusky light over the fields. I gasp when I see a string of lights making a path toward the barn. My heart beats a little faster, the smile on my face getting so big it makes my cheeks ache. Whatever Ranger's up to, he put a lot of time and effort into it.

I step inside the barn, where the animals have already settled in their stalls for the night. I look around for Ranger but don't see him anywhere. Then another piece of paper catches my eye. This one is taped to the ladder that leads to the hayloft. I move closer until I can read the words "Come up" scrawled on it.

"You bought me a fancy suit, and you're going to make me get it all dusty in the hayloft?" I complain, craning my neck, trying to see what he has going on up there.

His warm chuckle echoes down. "Just come up."

I grumble playfully. I don't care about getting the suit dirty. That's why dry cleaning was invented. Besides, life's too short for pristine clothes. When I reach the top of the ladder, I'm greeted by more lights, strung up all around the loft, casting a beautiful glow over the space. Ranger has shoved the hay bales to the sides, leaving a large, open space in the center for a folding table and two chairs. He must've gotten them up here, using the hay hoist. Ranger's standing beside the table with a grin.

When we built the barn, I insisted we put in a latched window that opens up like a skylight. I'll admit, I was having fantasies of a thrilling, romantic roll in the hay at the time. And I'm not disappointed by how breathtaking the view is from here. The pink-and-orange-streaked sky looks like someone painted it just for us.

Ranger holds out a hand, beckoning me over. "In case you were wondering, *this* is our first official date."

"It's..." I dart my eyes from the meal laid out on the table to the tailored suit he's looking all kinds of edible in. "Wow."

"Exactly the reaction I was hoping for." He kisses my cheek and pulls out a chair for me.

One look at the plate tells me he made my favorite: eggplant parmesan and a heaping amount of garlic bread. "This is incredible. I can't believe you did all this." I take a bite of the bread and groan happily. "It's so good," I mumble around a full mouth.

He laughs. "I wanted to do something special for you. I'm glad you like it."

"I'm speechless."

We both dig into our food, the conversation flowing effortlessly as we enjoy the delicious meal. The sunset outside fades to a dark sky, stars twinkling to life one at a time until there's a blanket of them overhead and our plates are empty.

"How did it go with the contractor today?" he asks, and I sigh.

"As badly as I feared. It's going to cost a lot more to rebuild than what my insurance is going to pay out. I can build the barn myself, I guess, but even then, I'm going to have to majorly downsize. It wouldn't be a big deal if it weren't for all the dogs. I guess my best option is to go with a smaller house and take on only one or two dogs to train at a time from now on so I won't be tripping over them."

He frowns, and I wonder what he's thinking.

"My other choice would be to save up for a while until I have enough to rebuild properly, but that could take years," I go on, sighing and then trying to push away this helpless feeling that has no place ruining this perfect date he organized. "Why don't we dance?"

Ranger smirks. "I was hoping you'd ask." He picks up his phone and presses a few buttons until soft, instrumental music starts to play. Then he shoves his chair back and gets to his feet, offering me his hand to help me up.

"Such a gentleman tonight."

"Don't get too used to it," he jokes, leading me over near the skylight and pulling me into his arms.

I relax into him, following his lead as our bodies sway together slowly to the beat. He's put on quite a bit of muscle since we first met, and I definitely don't hate the way his new bulk feels against my body. We grin like fools, dancing and twirling under the starlight. I dramatically ask him to dip me, and he obliges, nearly dropping me before recovering at the last minute, pulling me laughing against his chest.

My whole body feels lighter than air, with the steady beat of his heart matching my own, our chests pressed together, and our foreheads touching as we both savor this beautiful moment.

"I love you." The words fall from my lips unintentionally, but they're too honest to take back, even if I could. Maybe it's too fast, maybe this is crazy, but I'm madly in love with this man.

To my relief, Ranger smiles. "I'm *so* in love with you." My heart does its best to beat right out of my chest, and as does his, galloping against his ribs. His hold on me tightens. "Stay here."

"What do you mean?" I pull back just enough so I can study his face. He can't mean forever, right? Moving in together is a huge commitment.

"Sell your land and stay here with me. We've already started fixing this place up together, and we can do more. We can make it all our own, grow old here together with a dozen ornery goats and all the dogs you want."

A nervous, giddy quiver rises in me. Is he serious? The expression on his face is earnest, but can this be real?

"You mean that? You don't think it's too fast?" I ask. "I don't want you to feel pressured or like we have to do this just because I'm in a bad situation with my house. I can figure things out with a place to stay, and we can take this at a more comfortable pace. I mean—"

He cuts me off with a kiss. "I don't feel rushed. Who cares if it's fast? I want you with me."

I search his face for any sign he's not being honest, that

he feels pressured to move things forward before he's ready. All I see is calm certainty and the same overwhelming love filling me up inside.

"Okay, I'll stay."

35

RANGER

He's staying. He loves me. It's still hard to wrap my head around, even though I see on his face he means it. Not that he would ever joke about something like this, but the love is radiating off his face in such a way that I wonder how I could've missed that before.

"I love you," I say. How *right* those words feel on my tongue.

His smile has never been so beautiful, and my heart flutters all over again. "I like hearing those words."

"I like saying them."

I've always laughed when couples got all lovey-dovey with each other because it seemed so cheesy and corny, and yet here I am, embracing it with all my might. A romantic dinner, slow dancing, and saying I love you... It's a Hallmark movie come true. Not that I'd ever choose those. My mom did, and so we were forced to watch them with her. Oh, the horror.

She's always been a sucker for a happy ending, and mine is happening right now. Only one thing is missing...

I take a deep breath. "I want to tell you about Alex..."

He nods instantly. Then he takes my hand, and we sit down in the hay, nice suits and all.

Where do I start? It still feels so raw in my head, in my heart, but Julian deserves the truth.

Julian raises our joined hands and presses a kiss on mine. "Take your time."

I sit in silence, searching for the right words. "We became friends the moment we met. He was a couple of years younger, new to the Rangers, and since he was under my command, I was tasked with showing him the ropes. Brooklyn, we called him, because he had a heavy New York accent. Pretty sure he played it up, but that was Alex. Always the clown, making jokes at the most inappropriate times to relieve the tension."

I can't help but smile as the memories flood me. We shared so many laughs, the two of us in stitches like teenagers over the crazy stunts he pulled.

"Underneath, he was a damn good soldier. Fearless. And when everyone else was asleep, I saw his other side... We'd talk about him growing up with a single mom and five siblings. How he learned to cope with dyslexia in school. And the Yankees. God, he was a die-hard Yankees fan..."

"That's why you wear a Yankees cap..." Julian says.

"Yeah. It was his. His mother sent it to me, at his request."

Julian frowned. "How could he have requested that ahead of time?"

Sweet summer child. "We're soldiers, baby." The word falls from my lips as if I've said it a million times before. "The Army requires us to have our affairs in order before we ship out. After our first tour together, he made some changes to his last wishes, and one of them was that he asked his mom to send me some of his personal effects."

"Did she know?"

"I didn't even know. I knew he was gay, and so did his mom. He'd told me he'd come out in high school, and obviously, I was fine with it, but he didn't shout it from the rooftops. The Army has changed, but being gay can still cause a backlash, especially in a special unit like the Rangers. But I didn't know..." My voice breaks. "I didn't know he was in love with me."

My throat is tight now, and every word hurts. "And I didn't know I was in love with him. Not until... Not until it was too late..."

Julian clenches my fingers, tears shimmering in his eyes. I love him all the more for it. Lesser men would've been jealous of a previous love, but not him.

"My unit was on a mission, and we walked straight into a trap. One moment, everything was fine, and the next he was dead. He got hit by a sniper. The bullet came out of nowhere. Clean shot. I'll always be grateful for that, that it was instant. But as I held him in my arms, I knew I had lost the man I loved..."

Julian doesn't say anything, and that means everything. No clichés can ever comfort me, but that he's with me in my pain and grief is enough. Just knowing I'm not alone.

I take a few minutes to compose myself. "At first, I stayed, but my CO quickly realized I was in no condition to serve, so he sent me home. It was supposed to be temporary, but after four months, I received an honorable discharge with the official diagnosis of PTSD. The Army shrink said that the unexpectedness of the attack was what messed me up. I'd had everything under control, and then he was ripped away from me, and that fucked up my sense of safety. That's why I have a hard time dealing with sudden, unexpected moves..."

Julian's face lights up with understanding. "That's what happened the first time you had an episode with me."

"Yeah. You went down all of a sudden, and my brain decided that you had been shot, even though I knew it wasn't true. It happened too fast to override that reaction."

"That makes total sense."

"I thought it was stupid. My whole life I had trained for the unexpected, and yet when it happened, I was unable to deal with it."

"Yeah, but it was much more than that. You lost the man you were in love with before you had the chance to tell him or even realize you loved him. That's not something you can train for."

I slowly nod, pushing out a deep sigh. "So I've finally come to accept. It's not so much the ambush that fucked with my head. It was the guilt afterward, all these bottled-up emotions I couldn't tell anyone. And that got even worse when I received his letter. His mom shipped it to me with the things he wanted me to have. All I could feel was this deep regret that I had never known, that we'd never even had the chance to kiss or hold hands. If only I hadn't been so blind to my feelings..."

A tear drips down Julian's cheek, and I brush it off with my thumb. "I'm sorry I'm making you cry."

Julian waves off my apology. "Was he afraid of how you'd react if he told you how he felt?"

"He wrote he was scared to lose our friendship and that he'd decided to wait until he was certain I felt the same way. And that if I was reading his letter, it meant he might never have had the chance, and that was okay too."

"Maybe he did know."

I frown. What does he mean? "How could he have?"

"Because of the way you looked at him, how you treated

him, how you acted around him. If he loved you, he would've picked up on it."

"Then why didn't he say anything?"

"Because he was waiting for you to be ready. He knew you always thought you were straight, so my guess is that he figured you needed more time...and he was willing to wait for you."

Why did that thought never even occur to me? Now that Julian has brought it up, it fills me, replacing guilt with something else. Joy. Gratitude. I'll be forever glad and grateful that I met Alex and that, for a few years, we were together, even if it was never in the way it could have been. And if Julian is right and Alex knew what he meant to me, he died knowing he was loved. And that changes everything.

My eyes well up, and then they spill over. The next second I'm in Julian's arms, and he's holding me while I cry. I bawl like a baby as I mourn what I lost, what could've been, while at the same time letting go and embracing my second chance at love.

"I promise I'll tell you I love you every chance I get," I whisper when I'm finally done, exhausted. This is not how I intended to end this date, and yet it seems strangely fitting. You can't fully embrace the future until you accept and let go of the past.

"And I'll say it right back as many times as you need to hear it until you believe it."

"I love you."

Julian kisses my tear-stained cheek. "I love you too."

36

JULIAN

After Ranger's emotional confession last night, we climbed down the ladder, went inside, stripped down, and crawled into bed. We both cried, and he kept apologizing for ruining our date, but if anything, it only made it more complete. Hearing he loves me was amazing, but watching the last brick fall out of the wall he had up when we met was everything. We kissed and held each other, talking in low voices until the sun came up. Then we both finally drifted off to sleep.

Waking up wrapped in Ranger's arms is better than anything I could dream up in a lifetime. I've been waking up with his body plastered against mine every day since the wildfire, but it feels different this morning.

His skin is warm against mine, our legs tangled, his half-hard cock resting against the curve of my ass as his slow, steady breath puffs against the back of my neck. We're done holding back with each other, done waiting for this affair to run its course, and knowing that is even better than his arms around me, and that's seriously saying something.

He gives a sleepy groan, his cock twitching against my butt.

"Why, good morning to you too," I tease, pressing back. As his erection throbs again, a ripple of desire runs through me, and my cock surges to life.

"What time is it?" he asks around a yawn.

"Too early, considering how late we were up." I don't have to look at a clock to know that; the heaviness of my body is making it loud and clear.

"We've got farm chores to do," he groans again. This time it isn't a sexy groan, and I can relate.

I harrumph, rolling over to tempt him to let the animals wait for another hour. They'll be fine. Annoyed, but fine.

"Hi." He chuckles, smiling when my head comes to rest on the pillow a few inches from his, my nose bumping his.

"Hi," I echo, matching his grin and hitching my leg over his. I scoot my body close enough to press my hot, hard arousal to his thigh and revel in the low moan that falls from his lips.

I rest my hand on the hard plane of his stomach, the wiry scratch of his body hair rough under my palms. I could happily lie here like this for the rest of eternity. Who needs food or water? Not me, that's for sure.

God, I'm sappy when I'm in love, and I'm not the least bit sorry about that.

"You know, I was thinking. Since you told me about your first love last night, it's only fair that I tell you about mine."

Both Ranger's eyebrows shoot up. "Oh? Does he happen to have a nipple piercing and devilishly good looks?"

"You are my forever love, but sadly, there was once another." I sigh dramatically, drawing little circles on his skin with my thumb, as goose bumps pebble my arms.

"Do tell."

"I was eight, and I looked forward to it every week—the man in the khaki shorts with the Australian accent wrestling crocodiles and teaching viewers like me all about wildlife and conservation."

"Uh, Steve Irwin?" He's clearly not sold on the appeal of the man.

"Yes. I know he was a little goofy looking and definitely too old for me, but I loved him nonetheless." I pretend to swoon, making Ranger laugh. His body jostles against mine from the sound. I laugh along with him, spurred on when he playfully tickles me.

Somewhere in the midst of the laughter, our mouths collide, our lips sliding slowly over each other. The kiss is like all the best parts of a lazy Sunday morning, warm and syrupy. We rock in sync, my cock bumping against his, groaning into each other's mouths when we press our erections fully together.

Ranger drags his fingers through my hair while I trail my hands up to his chest, teasing his peaked nipples with my thumbs and drawing another rich, desperate sound from him.

"You know what I love about sex with you?" he murmurs against my lips.

"Hopefully everything." I nip at his bottom lip and thrust my cock against his again. A flare of heat burns in the pit of my stomach, searing me from the inside out. My balls tighten, and my cock leaks.

"Without a doubt." He kisses along my chin, grazing my skin gently with his teeth. "But I really love how it's not always about getting straight to the main event. Like, when you fingered me and then jerked off. I feel stupid saying it, but I never knew something that was *real* sex could be so good."

"Penetration doesn't equal real sex." I think I've done a good job of proving that point since we first started fooling around. I like anal as much as the next person, but it's not the end all be all.

"I know. That's what I'm saying. *This*"—he thrusts against me, sucking a spot on my neck until I'm sure he's left a bruise—"this is incredible. It's everything."

"Well, it's not *everything*. For example, if you roll over, I'll happily show you what my tongue can do." I waggle my eyebrows.

He presses one more kiss to my lips, then turns onto his stomach. The eager smile on his lips before he buries his face in the pillow speaks volumes. I throw the covers out of the way and straddle him from behind, the same way I did the day I gave him the massage. Things are an entire world of different now, neither of us tentative with each other, and Ranger very much not a virgin anymore.

I knead his shoulders a little before leaning forward and pressing a kiss between his shoulder blades. I slot my cock between his ass cheeks, and he arches against me. Okay, so there's *one* thing he hasn't experienced yet, but if he wants to, I'm more than game.

I kiss my way down his back, leaving a trail of kisses along his spine. I grab his cheeks in my hands, massaging them as I work my way down. Ranger gasps and cants his hips. I dip my tongue into each of the dimples at the base of his spine and then playfully bite his butt cheek. He wiggles, and I kiss the spot all better before continuing my journey.

He tilts his hips up, spreading his legs wider when I part his cheeks, inviting me to drag my tongue over his tight pucker. I tease his hole with the tip of my tongue and then a long, wet lick with the flat of it.

Ranger lets out a muffled moan into the pillow, his hole

twitching against my tongue as I lick him again, lapping at him over and over until he's panting and groaning, thrusting his hips desperately. I hum, the sound vibrating over my tongue as I lick him open.

"Fuck, that's so good," he grunts.

"Do you want my cock? Do you want to know how it feels to come with me deep inside you?" I run my fingertips over his rim, just like I did with my tongue, and kiss the crease where his butt meets his thigh.

"Hell, yes," Ranger gasps. My cock jerks against the bed, and I grin into his skin.

He's wet enough from my spit that my finger slides in easily, his hole clenching around it, making my cock ache to feel the same.

His channel is scorching hot around my finger as I press it deeper inside, working it in and out until his hole softens enough that I can add a second and a third. His body trembles, and beads of sweat form along his back.

"Julian, please..."

37

RANGER

"Please," I repeat, not ashamed to beg. His tongue and finger make my body light up in a way I've never experienced before. I want him inside me. No, I need him. *Crave* him. And I'll do whatever it takes to get him to fill me up.

But he doesn't make me beg again. No, he hushes me with a soft *ssh*, his hand patting me reassuringly The familiar *schnick* of a bottle of lube opening is music to my ears, and bless him, he warms it up on his fingers before he brings them to my ass. To my hole, which is quivering as it waits for him.

His fingers press, then sink in deep, and a delicious burn spreads. A sting mixed with pleasure, and I moan as he pumps them slowly. I buck my hips, already seeking more, and he chuckles. "I thought you always prided yourself on your patience?"

"That was before this," I mumble into the pillow. "Before you showed me what I've missed all these years."

"I'll be as quick as I can, but this is your first time, and I don't want to hurt you, so bear with me, okay?"

He takes his time, fucking me with his fingers until they slide in with ease, and then he adds a third. That bites like a motherfucker again, but he's patient, waiting for me to breathe through the pain. Thank fuck for those yoga exercises.

By the time he's pumping three fingers in and out of my hole, I'm grunting, groaning, moaning, growling, every sound I didn't even know I could make. They're coming from the back of my throat and mingle with the wet *schlock* of his fingers inside me, his appreciative hums, and our panting breaths, creating a sexual concert.

"Turn around," he says, and I obey instantly. His eyes are dark, his face intense, and he's so goddamn beautiful it takes my breath away. He bends in and kisses me, deep and erotic, his tongue delving into my mouth as if it's there to stay.

My hips lift off the mattress, seeking something, my body's wordless plea for more of what we were doing, please and thank you.

Julian breaks off our kiss, a twinkle in his eyes. "I see how it is. You wanna move on to the main course."

I smile back sheepishly. "Sorry? It seems my body has a mind of its own. But that doesn't mean the...appetizers weren't delicious."

He grins. "Good save."

Then he leans back and grabs a packet from the nightstand. My heart skips a beat, but it's excitement, not fear or apprehension, that's thundering through me. He tears it open and quickly rolls on a condom, and I spread my legs wide. I'm ready for him. *So* ready.

He knee-walks closer, stretches on top of me, and presses against me. For a moment, I freeze. "Sshh, just relax," Julian whispers. "Let me in, baby..."

I focus on unclenching my muscles, and my ass

responds, losing its tension. He slips in, and my breath catches in my lungs. Holy shit, this is... A *lot*.

Is it possible his cock has grown in diameter? 'Cause it sure as fuck feels a lot bigger than it looks. I suck in air between my teeth, again fighting to stay relaxed. Julian waits, not moving a muscle as he watches me.

As soon as I manage to get my muscles under control, he thrusts gently and inches in deeper. And then my body finally gets the message that yes, this will grow into pleasure if we stop fighting it, and Julian sinks in all the way, filling me up inch by inch until his balls rest against my ass.

Liquid heat races up my spine, spreading out from my ass to my very fingertips, and god, this is ten times better than I could ever have imagined. My cock is fat and swollen between us, screaming for attention, but I ignore it for now. I want this to last.

Julian's eyes drill into mine as he rocks with slow, deep strokes that completely work me open. The last bit of pain drifts away, and all that remains is ecstasy, so intense my body is humming and vibrating. I've never felt this *alive*.

He kisses me again, starting slow, then speeding up until his tongue thrust in tandem with his cock. He's fucking my mouth and my ass, and all I can do is take it because I'm too overwhelmed to do anything but lie there and get used to this foreign but mind-blowing sensation of having someone *inside* me.

Julian keeps kissing me and making love to my ass, and my body heats up in new ways. At first, I'm slowly rocking against him, but then I jolt against him every time he thrusts, and oh fuck, that fires up my ass. How did I never know how many nerves I have there? Delicious nerves that ignite in the best way every time Julian's cock slides deep inside me, brushing what has to be my prostate until I'm whimpering.

"Julian," I groan, ready to beg all over again, though for what, I'm not sure. He hasn't stopped moving. His thrusts are steady, rhythmic, and his ragged breaths are in tune with mine. My chest is heaving, my cock is throbbing, and my whole body is screaming with need.

A violent shudder tears through me, and I can't resist anymore. I need to touch myself. My hand curls around my cock, and I squeeze the head firmly. Oh god. No way in hell can I keep going for much longer.

"Don't fight it. Let yourself come," Julian says hoarsely. "I want to watch you."

I release the tight hold I've had on myself and all but push up my ass to draw him in deeper while my hand is furiously jerking off my leaking cock. My balls clench tight, and my muscles stiffen in anticipation.

I can't keep my eyes open, no matter how much I want to. It's just too much. I'm hurtling toward the edge, and where I usually hover, I now dive straight off the cliff. I scream as I come, my cock pulsing in my hand as the cum spurts out. For a second or two, three, I can't breathe, and then I suck in the air, lightheaded from the force of my orgasm.

I collapse onto the mattress, boneless, too wiped out to even move a muscle. Julian kisses me quickly, but before I can respond to the touch of his lips, he gently pulls out. Did he come? Was I so absorbed in my own release that I missed that?

But no, he kneels between my legs and pulls off the condom. And as I lie there like a puddle of happy, satisfied man, he meets my eyes and fists himself. He smiles as he jacks himself off, fast and hard, and then he sprays all over me, hitting my chest, my belly, and even my chin.

I lazily bring my fingers to my chin and swipe off his cum. And while he sits watching me, his chest heaving with heavy breaths, I lift my fingers to my mouth and lick them off. "Breakfast," I say with a wink. Julian bursts out laughing, rolling on top of me again, smearing our combined cum all over our bodies, and kisses me.

I guess the animals will have to wait a little longer.

38

RANGER

I'm working on expanding the fencing so the horses have more space when Benny barks. That's such a rare occurrence that I immediately put my tools down and check to see what's happening.

Julian isn't home, and I'm not expecting him back anytime soon, so it's not him. Besides, Benny wouldn't bark for that. He had a meeting with a Realtor to start the process of selling his land. She expected it to be an easy sale, despite the fire damage, since he owns a sizable plot. And after that, he was gonna run some other errands. Plenty of things to do after your house burns to the ground, unfortunately.

A strange car is pulling up in the driveway, and I frown. Who's that?

I recognize him as soon as he opens the door and carefully gets out, Mr. Sherman, the man who came to my aid in the grocery store and who owned this house before I bought it.

"Let's go say hello," I tell Benny, who follows me like the good boy he is. He really has been trained well.

"Good morning, Mr. Sherman," I say when we're close.

"Good morning, Ranger. I thought I'd stop by for a moment, if this is a convenient time for you."

I'm not sure why he wants to stop by, but he was nice enough last time we met, so why not? "I was due a break anyway. Can I get you something to drink?"

"Just a glass of water, please. The days where I could drink sodas and sweet tea in unlimited quantities are over, I'm afraid."

"Have a seat." I gesture at the rockers on the shaded porch. "I'll be right back."

I bring out water for him and a Coke for myself, then sit on the other chair.

"How have you been?" Mr. Sherman asks.

I chuckle. "Would you like the polite version or the truth?"

"Always the truth. I'm too old to waste my time with pretending and platitudes."

"That sounds like heaven. Never had much tolerance for it myself." I take a few gulps of my Coke, the ice-cold liquid wonderfully soothing for my parched throat. "I'm much better than the previous time we met."

"I can tell. You look better."

I love how direct and honest he is. "I gained back the weight I lost. I'm also sleeping much better, and I have more energy."

"You painted the house."

I wince. "I did. I know it was long overdue, but—"

"None of that, now," he cuts me off. "That wasn't implied criticism. I'm just happy to see the house being restored to its former glory."

"It's a good house, with great bones and a lot of potential. And it's..." I search for words. "It's a friendly house. It feels warm and welcome. Even when I didn't take care of it, it wasn't judging me. I know, I sound like a crackpot..."

"No, not at all. I know exactly what you mean. This house..." He lets out a long sigh. "I built this for Doris after the war. We were high school sweethearts, and she was devastated when I was sent to Vietnam... Even more when I signed up for two more tours. But I excelled at being a soldier and made it to platoon sergeant. All I wanted was to keep those young boys safe. But when I got back, I wasn't the same..."

"War changes you," I say softly.

"You'd know all about that."

"I do."

"Doris wasn't sure if she still wanted to marry me, if she was safe with me, and so I made her a promise. I asked her to give me a year to prove to her that even though I wasn't the same man, I was still worthy of her love."

Oh my god, he's gonna make me cry, isn't he? I feel an epic love story coming.

"In that year, I built this house, and I poured my love for her into every nail, every brick, every shingle on the roof. And working with my hands helped me to make peace with my demons as well. After that year, she agreed to marry me, and we got married the week after."

Yup, my eyes are getting all moist, and I have to clear my throat before I can speak. "That explains why the house is so welcoming."

"We had forty-eight wonderful years here and raised two daughters who still make me proud. But after Doris passed away... She was never sick, but one day, her heart just stopped, so it was mercifully quick. I couldn't live here without her, not by myself. I wanted to sell, but I turned down several buyers because they weren't right. Until you."

"You turned down buyers? Why?"

"Because this house is a blessing, and it needed to go to someone who deserved it. You do."

"Mr. Sherman…" I swallow. "I'm not sure that I'm—"

"You are. You're worthy and deserving, Ranger. Of all the good things in life. The fact that you doubt that, that you feel different, is your survivor's guilt talking. You're alive, and some of your friends are not, but that doesn't mean you shouldn't be happy. You'll carry some of that burden with you forever, but don't allow it to weigh you down."

I'm crying for real now. I have to tell myself that it's good and healthy and normal because that ugly voice that says tough-ass soldiers like me don't cry is speaking up again. "I want to be happy, but it's not easy. Will it ever get easier?"

"I promise it will."

"I have a boyfriend." I wait a beat to brace myself for his reaction, but all he does is smile at me. "He's the most amazing person I could ever meet, and for some reason, he loves me. I want to be happy with him, and right now, I'm doing well, but what if that doesn't last?"

"Does he know about your PTSD?"

I nod.

"Then that's enough. Your happiness won't last forever, Ranger. You will have setbacks, but you'll crawl back up, and over time, those days will become less, and you'll find yourself having far, far more good days than bad."

He's not sugarcoating it, and that means everything to me. "Were you officially diagnosed with PTSD?"

"No. War trauma for soldiers was still a taboo. I didn't get that label until much later, but I knew that in hindsight, that's what I have."

"Have? Not had?"

He smiles gently. "It never fully goes away. It'll always be there, and even now, fifty years later, I do have the occasional triggers where I'm back in that jungle all of a sudden, holding dying men in my arms."

Silence hangs between us, but it's a good silence, one shared in mutual understanding.

"Thank you," I say finally. "Thank you for selling me your house, but even more for sharing your story. It's given me hope."

"You're a good man, Ranger, and you deserve all the happiness in life. I pray the house I built will be as much a blessing for you and your family as it was for me and mine."

"Would you like a tour to see what I've done so far in fixing it up?"

His eyes light up. "I'd love to. I think I spotted some new outbuildings?"

"Yeah, I built two barns. My boyfriend's house burned down in the fire, so he and his animals moved in here. Five horses, four chickens, two goats, one dog...and a partridge in a pear tree."

Mr. Sherman laughs at my joke, which was, I'll admit, arguably lame. But maybe I'm getting better at it than I realized. I show him the progress I'm making on renovating the bathroom, and then he inspects the new barns and fences. "You're doing a great job. It makes me happy to see this place alive again."

"You can stop by any time," I tell him, and his smile widens.

"Be careful what you say to an old man. I may be dropping in a lot more than you'd counted on."

He's lonely. I don't know why that thought never occurred to me, but it's crystal clear to me. "Where do your daughters live?"

"My oldest is in South Korea, where her husband is stationed. My youngest is a surgical resident in Atlanta."

His voice rings with pride but also with underlying sadness. "And you're here," I say softly.

"She offered to move me to Atlanta to be closer to her, but I can't leave this town. Doris is buried here, and I have too many good memories. Besides, she's busy with her career and a wonderful girlfriend."

Well, that explains the lack of judgment when I told him about Julian. "Mr. Sherman, I mean it when I say you're welcome here anytime."

"You'd better clear that with your boyfriend first, Ranger. And please, call me Marvin."

I grin. "My boyfriend collects stray animals. Pretty sure he's fine with a stray human."

"In that case, do you need some help with that fence?"

SIX MONTHS LATER
JULIAN

A wet nose on my foot startles me out of a rather pleasant dream I was having about my boyfriend. With a grin on my face, I roll over, reaching for Ranger without opening my eyes. Unfortunately, my plan to re-enact the dream is thwarted by his very cold and empty side of the bed.

I grumble, opening my eyes and yawning. I don't have long to mentally complain about my lonely predicament because PP takes it upon herself to crawl up the bed and start licking my cheek.

"Yes, it's good to see you too." I yawn again, dodging when she tries to stick her tongue right into my mouth. Not exactly the French kiss I was hoping for this morning. I indulge in a few minutes of husky cuddles, then drag myself out of bed and go in search of my man.

My man. I still get a giddy smile on my face every time I think of him. Six months living together and we're still very much in the honeymoon phase, but I have every confidence we're building a relationship that's going to last long beyond these fluffy, wonderful early years.

As soon as I step out of the bedroom, the smell of pancakes wafts to my nose. I shuffle to the kitchen and find Ranger standing over the stove, holding a spatula, the frilly pink apron I bought him as a joke tied around his neck. Benny thumps his tail against the floor but doesn't move from his spot next to his person. I wrap my arms around him from behind, pressing my morning erection against his ass and kissing the back of his neck.

"I missed you in bed this morning."

"I can feel that." He chuckles and grinds his ass back against me, flipping the pancake that's in the pan. It has chocolate chips, naturally, just like all the pancakes Ranger makes for me these days.

"Sorry I overslept. You wore me out last night." I nip playfully at his earlobe, then reach past him and snag a strip of fake-on (aka meatless bacon) off the plate next to the stove.

"I let you sleep. The puppies started barking, and I figured if I got up to let them out and feed them, then you could get a little extra rest this morning."

"Thank you, that was sweet of you."

"No problem. You know I love the babies."

I took some time to get settled here before accepting a new litter of pups to train. This batch is a bunch of rambunctious but extremely smart border collies. They're only ten weeks, and we've already got them potty trained and responding to the basic commands. Benny loves them. PP is, as always, less than impressed.

"You can't get attached," I remind him.

"I know, but they're too cute not to love."

"Believe me, I know. Letting them go after a year of bonding with them is always the hardest part." I pat Benny on the head. Ranger plates our breakfast, and I bring both plates to the table while he pours us each a glass of orange juice. It's terribly domestic, and I couldn't be happier if I tried.

"Do you have any jobs scheduled today?" I ask. A few months ago, Ranger started his own small handyman business, basically putting his number up on a few apps and making his own simple website. After a few months of hemming and hawing about it, he also signed up for night classes in construction management so he can work on getting a contractor certification.

"Nothing as of now, but who knows what could roll in later?"

He still struggles some days, of course. There's no magic fix for PTSD after all, but he smiles more often than not now, and I can tell that having a purpose has made him feel more like himself again. Between that and how busy I keep him around here, I wouldn't be surprised if sometimes he still wishes for his old days of peace and quiet.

Ranger smiles at me, reaching across the table and taking my hand in his. My heart gives a silly little flutter like it always does when he touches me, and I bump my foot against his. I'm pretty sure if Benny and PP could roll their eyes at our disgusting display of schmoopieness, they would.

Once we've finished eating, I get dressed, and we head outside to do our morning feedings and stall mucking. As always, Doc brays loudly, banging on his stall door until I fill his trough with alfalfa hay, which he then happily munches on without so much as a thank-you.

Butler's stall is next, or I should say Butler's and Buddy's. I looked high and low for Buddy's owner, putting up posters everywhere, posting on social media, and even letting all the local shelters know just in case, but whoever he used to belong to never came looking for him. It all worked out for the best because Butler has never been happier.

Gone are the days of pool noodles on his horns to keep him from injuring me. I stop at their stall with their flakes of feed, and Butler bleats softly and gently nibbles my hand as I reach over the stall wall and put the feed hay into the trough. If I'd known that all it would take to make him like me was to find him a cute boyfriend, I would've done that ages ago.

Speaking of happy, we also built a tiny house on the property for Marvin Sherman to live here. Neither of us liked the idea of him being all alone. Everything's better with family, whether it's by blood or by heart.

Ranger and I have a great system down for finishing morning chores, and there's something nice about having someone to shovel horse shit with. If there's anything more romantic than that, I don't know what it is.

I admire the bulge of Ranger's biceps as he dumps a heap into the wheelbarrow, and smile.

"What?" he asks when he catches me looking.

I shrug. "Just thinking about how lucky I am to have such a sexy, incredible partner."

He leans the shovel against the wheelbarrow and strides over to me. Then he yanks me into his arms and kisses me fiercely.

"I'm the lucky one," he mumbles against my lips, sneaking a hand down and squeezing my butt.

"I guess we're both lucky, then. Lucky to be so crazy in love with each other."

"Without a doubt," he agrees. "Today, tomorrow, and forever."

"Forever," I echo, kissing his lips one more time and thanking every lucky star in the sky for this man.

The End

∼

WANNA READ the story of Lucky and his men? Start reading **Heart** today. Or start with **Rebel**, the first book in the Ballsy Boys series.

BOOKS BY K.M. NEUHOLD

Stand Alones
Change of Heart

Love Logic
Rocket Science
Four Letter Word

Four Bears Construction
Caulky
Nailed
Hardwood
Screwed

Heathens Ink
Rescue Me
Going Commando
From Ashes
Shattered Pieces
Inked in Vegas
Flash Me

Inked
- Unraveled
- Uncomplicated
- Unexpected

Replay
- Face the Music
- Play it by Ear
- Beat of Their Own Drum
- Strike a Chord

Working Out The Kinks
- Stay
- Heel

Ballsy Boys
- Rebel
- Tank
- Heart
- Campy
- Pixie

Kinky Boys
- Daddy
- Ziggy

Short and Sweet Stand Alones
- That One Summer
- Always You

BOOKS BY NORA PHOENIX

🎧 indicates book is also available as audio book

White House Men

A romantic suspense series set in the White House that combines romance with suspense, a dash of kink, and all the feels.

- **Press** (rivals fall in love in an impossible love)
- **Friends** (friends to lovers between an FBI and a Secret Service agent)

Perfect Hands Series

Raw, emotional, both sweet and sexy, with a solid dash of kink, that's the Perfect Hands series. All books can be read as standalones.

- **Firm Hand** (daddy care with a younger daddy and an older boy) 🎧
- **Gentle Hand** (sweet daddy care with age play) 🎧

- **Naughty Hand** (a holiday novella to read after Firm Hand and Gentle Hand) 🎧
- **Slow Hand** (a Dom who never wanted to be a Daddy takes in two abused boys) 🎧
- **Healing Hand** (a broken boy finds the perfect Daddy) 🎧

No Shame Series

If you love steamy MM romance with a little twist, you'll love the No Shame series. Sexy, emotional, with a bit of suspense and all the feels. Make sure to read in order, as this is a series with a continuing storyline.

- **No Filter** 🎧
- **No Limits** 🎧
- **No Fear** 🎧
- **No Shame** 🎧
- **No Angel** 🎧

And for all the fun, grab the **No Shame box set** 🎧 which includes all five books plus exclusive bonus chapters and deleted scenes.

Irresistible Omegas Series

An mpreg series with all the heat, epic world building, poly romances (the first two books are MMMM and the rest of the series is MMM), a bit of suspense, and characters that will stay with you for a long time. This is a continuing series, so read in order.

- **Alpha's Sacrifice** 🎧
- **Alpha's Submission** 🎧
- **Beta's Surrender** 🎧

- **Alpha's Pride** 🎧
- **Beta's Strength** 🎧
- Omega's Protector
- Alpha's Obedience
- Omega's Power
- Beta's Love
- Omega's Truth

Or grab *the first box set*, which contains books 1-3 plus exclusive bonus material and *the second box set*, which has books 4-6 and exclusive extras.

Ballsy Boys Series

Sexy porn stars looking for real love! Expect plenty of steam, but all the feels as well. They can be read as stand-alones, but are more fun when read in order.

- **Ballsy** (free prequel)
- **Rebel** 🎧
- **Tank** 🎧
- **Heart** 🎧
- **Campy** 🎧
- **Pixie** 🎧

Or grab *the box set*, which contains all five books plus an exclusive bonus novella!

Kinky Boys Series

Super sexy, slightly kinky, with all the feels.

- **Daddy** 🎧
- **Ziggy** 🎧

Ignite Series

An epic dystopian sci-fi trilogy (one book out, two more to follow) where three men have to not only escape a government that wants to jail them for being gay but aliens as well. Slow burn MMM romance.

- **Ignite** 🎧
- **Smolder** 🎧
- **Burn** 🎧

Now also available in a *box set* 🎧, which includes all three books, bonus chapters, and a bonus novella.

Stand Alones

I also have a few stand alones, so check these out!

- **Professor Daddy** (sexy daddy kink between a college prof and his student. Age gap, no ABDL) 🎧
- **Out to Win** (two men meet at a TV singing contest) 🎧
- **Captain Silver Fox** (falling for the boss on a cruise ship) 🎧
- **Coming Out on Top** (snowed in, age gap, size difference, and a bossy twink) 🎧

MORE ABOUT K.M. NEUHOLD

Author K.M.Neuhold is a complete romance junkie, a total sap in every way. She started her journey as an author in new adult, MF romance, but after a chance reading of an MM book she was completely hooked on everything about lovely- and sometimes damaged- men finding their Happily Ever After together.

She has a strong passion for writing characters with a lot of heart and soul, and a bit of humor as well. And she fully admits that her OCD tendencies of making sure every side character has a full backstory will likely always lead to every book having a spin-off or series.

When she's not writing she's a lion tamer, an astronaut, and a superhero...just kidding, she's likely watching Netflix and snuggling with her husky while her amazing husband brings her coffee.

Stalk Me
Website: authorkmneuhold.com
Email: kmneuhold@gmail.com
Instagram: @KMNeuhold

BookBub: https://www.bookbub.com/authors/k-m-neuhold

Twitter: @KMNeuhold

Facebook group: https://www.facebook.com/groups/neuholdsnerds

MORE ABOUT NORA PHOENIX

Would you like the long or the short version of my bio?

The short? You got it.

I write steamy gay romance books and I love it. I also love reading books. Books are everything.

How was that?

A little more detail? Gotcha.

I started writing my first stories when I was a teen...on a freaking typewriter. I still have these, and they're adorably romantic. And bad, haha. Fear of failing kept me from following my dream to become a romance author, so you can imagine how proud and ecstatic I am that I finally overcame my fears and self doubt and did it. I adore my genre because I love writing and reading about flawed, strong men who are just a tad broken..but find their happy ever after anyway.

My favorite books to read are pretty much all MM/gay romances as long as it has a happy end. Kink is a plus... Aside from that, I also read a lot of nonfiction and not just books on writing. Popular psychology is a favorite topic of mine and so are self help and sociology.

Hobbies? Ain't nobody got time for that. Just kidding. I love traveling, spending time near the ocean, and hiking. But I love books more.

Come hang out with me in my Facebook Group Nora's Nook where I share previews, sneak peeks, freebies, fun stuff, and much more: https://www.facebook.com/groups/norasnook/

My weekly newsletter not only gives you updates, exclusive content, and all the inside news on what I'm working on, but also lists the best new releases, 99c deals, and freebies in gay romance for that weekend. Load up your Kindle for less money! Sign up here: http://www.noraphoenix.com/newsletter/

You can also stalk me on Twitter: @NoraFromBHR

On Instagram:

https://www.instagram.com/nora.phoenix/

On Bookbub:

https://www.bookbub.com/profile/nora-phoenix

Or become my patron on Patreon: https://www.patreon.com/noraphoenix

Printed in Great Britain
by Amazon